guard rooster

To carington

from zuhair Merchant

guard rooster

XULON **PRESS**

Xulon Press
2301 Lucien Way #415
Maitland, FL 32751
407.339.4217
www.xulonpress.com

Printed in the United States of America.

ISBN: 9781545611548

chapter one

ittle Stevie was little. Even at twelve years old he was no bigger than a third grader. Little Stevie's dad, Big Steve, always told Little Stevie to jump into his pocket and go for a ride on the Super Strip. The Super Strip was the half mile of road with a grocery store, a dollar store, a hardware store, a drugstore, The Diner, a gas station and the City Hall. "You can just sit in my hip pocket and see all the stuff there is to see on The Super Strip," Big Steve would say and then rub Little Stevie's head. Little Stevie had thick yellow hair that always fell back into place after it was messed up, so Little Stevie didn't mind if Big Steve rubbed his head.

Little Stevie was smart too. He made good grades in school and he always did his homework. He listened to his teachers and always said "yes ma'am" and "no ma'am" as well as "yes sir" and "no sir" to all of the grown ups. Little Stevie was always nice to everybody and everybody liked him, except for the school bullies. They didn't like anybody that was smarter than they were, which was everybody, so they didn't like anybody. There were four or five of *them* and they didn't even like each other. They *really* didn't like Little Stevie.

chapter one

Little Stevie liked to help others with their class work as long as the teacher said it was okay. It wasn't allowed at test time though, nobody was allowed to talk during exams or tests.

One day during a math quiz, a kid named Barney looked over at Little Stevie. "Pst!" Barney whispered. Barney was one of the school bullies. "Pst! Little Stevie! What's the answer to number three?" Little Stevie didn't even look at Barney, he just kept on working on his own quiz. "Pst!" Barney made the sound again. "Little Stevie! What's the answer to number three?" Barney repeated the question. Little Stevie always tried to do the right thing so he looked over at Barney and told him to be quiet. "Ssh!" Little Stevie hissed with his finger on his lips. Little Stevie wasn't afraid of Barney the bully, even though he was so little, but Barney was mean and he was getting really angry. "Pst! What is the answer to number three?" Little Stevie was about to tell Barney to be quiet again when the teacher heard them. "Is there a problem Stevie?" She asked. "No ma'am." Little Stevie said.

"Well, let's be quiet until everybody finishes the test. Okay?"

"Yes ma'am." He said. Little Stevie looked over at Barney again and Barney asked Stevie again. "What's the answer to number three?"

"Barney!" The teacher said loudly. "What is the problem?"

"Nuttin!" Barney answered.

"Then why are you talking?"

Barney just sat there. "Uh, uh, uh," was all he could say at first. "Little Stevie was asking me the answer to number three!" Barney lied.

"Seriously Barney?" The teacher asked, but she knew he was lying. "How bout it, Stevie, is that true?"

Little Stevie always told the truth. "No ma'am."

"I didn't think so. Barney, go sit in the hall and finish your quiz!"

"Aw! I didn't do nuttin!" Barney said.

"You told a lie and you were talking during a test! Now go and sit in the hall!"

Barney leaned over and told Little Stevie that he was going to get him after school. "You meet me behind the cafeteria after school Little Stevie, and I'll give you a knuckle sandwich!" Barney whispered.

"Out in the hall, *now* Barney!" The teacher said, and Barney went out into the hall to finish his test.

After math class was over with Barney told his bully buddies that Little Stevie got him in trouble. But Little Stevie didn't do anything wrong, Barney was just mad because Little Stevie wouldn't help him cheat on a test. The bullies didn't care, they just wanted somebody to pick on, and Little Stevie was their victim of the day. Little Stevie acted like he wasn't scared, but they were all bigger than he was, so there was no way that he was going to meet them behind the cafeteria after school. Little Stevie was too smart for that kind of nonsense.

When school was over for the day Little Stevie waited with the other car riders in the cafeteria for their moms or dads to come and pick them up. While he was waiting he saw Barney and his bully buddies outside one of the cafeteria windows. Barney made a fist at Little Stevie and then turned to get on his bus. Little Stevie still acted like he wasn't scared, but he knew that if the bullies ever caught him away from school with no grown-ups around, they would probably beat him up.

Little Stevie's mom arrived to pick him up and she knew there was something bothering him. "What's wrong Stevie?" His mom asked.

"I don't want to talk about it." Little Stevie said.

"Are you sure?" His mom asked. "Sometimes it helps if you talk about things." Little Stevie's mom knew that he got picked on from time to time because he was so little, but Stevie never wanted to talk about it. "Okay." His mom said. "But if you want to talk about it later…" Little Stevie didn't say anything.

Later that evening at the supper table Big Steve asked Little Stevie how his day was and Little Stevie didn't say a word. He just looked at his mom and dropped his head.

"What happened at school today?" Big Steve asked but Little Stevie didn't say a word. Big Steve looked at Mom and she told him. "I'm not sure but I think that gang of hooligans in school is picking on your son again, but he doesn't want to talk about it."

Right about then Little Stevie wanted to melt like a popsicle and ooze onto the floor and right under the door.

"*Stevie!*" Big Steve said. "Tell me what happened today."

Little Stevie remained silent, so Big Steve got a little louder. "Stevie, tell me what happened at school today!"

"It's not just today, it's every day!" Little Stevie finally burst out. "There's this kid named Barney and he doesn't like me, and everyday he tries to pick a fight with me, *and* he's the biggest kid in school, *and* he would kill me!" Little Stevie went on and on. "I wish I was big like you daddy, and then nobody would ever bother me again!" He felt like crying but he didn't, he held it in.

Big Steve looked at Mom and shook his head. "I guess I'll have to go down to the school tomorrow and speak with the principal and…"

"No!" Little Stevie said. "That will only make things worse." Big Steve scratched his head. "Well, what should we do about it Stevie? What do you want to do?" He asked Little Stevie. "I don't *know*…" Then Stevie's eyes lit up like they did when he was thinking. "Teach me how to box Daddy." Little Stevie said. Mom looked up and rolled her eyes. She knew where this was going. Little Stevie had talked about it before. Big Steve rubbed his chin thoughtfully.

"Teach me some of your old boxing moves and I can do a rope a dope on Barney the bully." Little Stevie didn't know what a "rope a dope" was, but he had heard his dad say it before so it sounded good to him.

"I suppose I could show you a thing or two, you know, from my days as a Golden Gloves boxer." Big Steve told his son. Big Steve had been an amateur boxer as a teenager and had participated in several Golden Glove tournaments.

"Oh yea!" Little Stevie said with excitement in his voice.

"I guess we could start tomorrow." Big Steve said. "But it's only for self defense, not for going out and picking fights. You understand?"

"Yes sir." Little Stevie answered respectfully.

***

The next day Big Steve began showing Little Stevie some boxing moves and a few punches. He showed Little Stevie how to "stick and move" and how to "bob and weave" so he could avoid getting hit in case somebody decided to take a swing at him. Little Stevie's mom wasn't happy about the idea of her son fighting, but she realized that he needed to know how to defend himself just in case, so she didn't protest. "I don't like the idea of my baby fighting and maybe getting hurt," was all she said about it.

On the way to school the next morning Little Stevie was still excited about what Big Steve had taught him and he already felt like he take care of himself if he got picked on that day. When he arrived at school however, and saw Barney the Bully along with the other bullies, he wasn't so sure of himself. They were so *big*! His mom saw the change in his attitude and asked him if he would like to take the day off from school and go back home. "No ma'am." Little Stevie said. "I might as well get it over with."

"Are you sure?" Mom asked.

"I'll be okay mom." Little Stevie told her and got out of the car. Mom watched Stevie go inside the cafeteria and she watched until he was out of sight. Then she pulled out of the school parking lot with a sure enough "worried mom look" all over her face. Little Stevie went and sat down with his friends at one of the tables in the cafeteria. It wasn't until then that he noticed Barney the Bully staring at him from across the cafeteria. Barney was sitting with the other bullies and they were all looking at Little Stevie. Little Stevie tried not to look at them but couldn't help glancing over across the cafeteria. Barney made another fist at Little Stevie but Little Stevie just ignored the gesture and looked away. The bell to go to class was ringing anyhow.

Little Stevie finished his first period class work long before class was over with and began daydreaming. He imagined himself boxing in a Golden Gloves tournament just like his dad had done. He pictured his hand being raised in the center of a boxing ring, and he imagined that it was Barney the Bully he had just whipped the tar out of, right after taking care of the bully's bud-dies, one by one.

"And your winner...Little Stevie!" He could hear over the roar of the crowd. "Little Stevie! Little Stevie!" He could still hear his name being called. "Little Stevie!" He jumped, startled out of his daydream by his best friend Donald. "It's time to go to second period."

"Oh!" He said. "Let's go!" When the two of them left the class-room and went into the hallway Little Stevie saw something out of the corner of his eye. It was Barney, and Little Stevie knew that Barney was up to something. Little Stevie looked down and he saw Barney's foot just in time to avoid being tripped. Little Stevie hopped with ease over Barney's foot and kept on walking. He didn't miss a step. Barney just stood there with his mouth open wide enough to stick that big ole foot of his in.

During recess after lunch, Barney and one of his bully bud-dies began calling Little Stevie names like chicken and scaredy cat. They were following him around and making clucking noises and flapping their arms like chickens. It was very annoying to Little Stevie as well as his friends so Little Stevie came up with a plan to get rid of them for the remainder of recess. Little Stevie knew that before recess was over with the custodians would start to clean the cafeteria. There were two custodians, Freddie and Charlie, and Stevie had made friends with both of them way back in kindergarten and he knew their schedule better than they did. Little Stevie also knew that students were not allowed in the cafeteria once lunch was over with because they would be in Freddie and Charlie's way. The floors of the cafeteria would also be wet from being mopped and students could slip and fall so that was another reason students weren't allowed in there after lunch. Freddie and Charlie always took a short break after mopping the floors to let them dry, so there wouldn't be anybody in the cafeteria for a few minutes during recess and Little Stevie knew that too.

"Okay Barney!" Little Stevie spun around so suddenly that Barney and his bully buddies were startled enough to stop acting like brain-dead chickens for a second. "I'm going to the restroom, then I'll see you in the cafeteria and we'll see who's chicken!"

"What?" Donald stopped in his tracks. "Stevie you can't..."

Little Stevie looked away from Barney and winked at Donald. Donald nodded and winked back at Little Stevie, knowing that Little Stevie had a plan.

"But we're not supposed to go in the cafeteria after lunch." Barney told Little Stevie.

"What are you saying Barney?" Little Stevie asked. "Are you chicken?" But he knew that Freddie and Charlie would return soon. Little Stevie began clucking like a chicken himself and flapping his arms like he had wings. "Who's the chicken now?" He asked and looked at Barney's buddies. They all looked at

Barney and Barney was looking all around at all the kids that were waiting for him to say or do something.

"No, I'm not the chicken! You're the chicken!" Barney finally said. "We'll be there! Won't we?" Barney nudged one of his bully buddies with an elbow.

"Uh, yea!" He said.

Little Stevie walked away in the direction of the gymnasium entrance to go to the restroom. He knew that Freddie and Charlie would be returning to the cafeteria in just a couple of minutes, but Barney didn't know it. Little Stevie went into the gymnasium, used the restroom and came back outside just in time to see Barney and his bully buddies being led away to the principal's office. "Well, that's that." Little Stevie said to himself. "For the rest of the day at least!" Barney and his buddies got detention for the remainder of the day.

***

After school that day, Little Stevie hooked up with his best bud Donald and they stood near the end of Little Stevie's driveway and talked for a while.

"So, do you think Barney and the rest of those goofballs are gonna try and get even with you for the cafeteria thing?" Donald asked Little Stevie.

"Yea. Probably." Little Stevie replied calmly, like he wasn't worried at all. "Even if I get punched in the nose though," He continued. "It'll only hurt for a minute. And it was worth it!"

"You got that right!" Donald exclaimed.

"You'd better watch your back too." Stevie told Donald. "Barney will probably…"

"Stevie!" It was mom. "Time for supper!"

"I gotta go." Little Stevie said.

"Yea, me too." Said Donald. "I'll see you tomorrow."

"Okay."

At the dinner table Big Steve noticed that Little Stevie was in much better spirits than he was a couple of days earlier.

"How was school today Stevie?" Big Steve asked his son. Little Stevie smiled when he remembered the look on Barney's face as he was being led to the principal's office for being in the cafeteria after lunch.

"It was a good day Dad." Little Stevie said and began having images in his head about being in a boxing ring again and beating the brakes off of Barney the Bully.

""After supper, later on this evening we'll put the gloves on and train for a little while." Big Steve told his son.

Little Stevie's eyes lit up. "Yes, yes!" He said twice. Then he raised his hands in a victory sign and shouted, "I am the greatest!" Little Stevie had seen his dad do that once or twice and he thought it was cool.

"Hey!" Big Steve said to Little Stevie. "You wanna go fishing on Saturday? I've got nothing to do, so why don't you and I take a little walk down to the creek and catch us some brim!"

"Sounds like a winner to me!" Little Stevie replied. He and his dad hadn't been fishing in a while and Little Stevie had always liked sitting on the creek bank with his dad early in the morning catching brim and sometimes catfish too.

"That's what we'll do then, early Saturday morning! Okay?"
"Right Dad!"

Saturday morning rolled around and Little Stevie was out of bed and dressed before his dad woke up and he turned on the coffee maker so the coffee would be ready when Big Steve got up. Fifteen minutes later, Big Steve was up, dressed and sipping on a cup of fresh hot coffee while Little Stevie helped out by checking to see if they had everything that they would need. Little Stevie had a mental list and after he double checked everything, they were on their way. Big Steve carried the fishing rods and the tackle box while Little Stevie threw a backpack full of bottled water and snacks over his shoulder.

"We good?" Big Steve asked and looked at the backpack on Little Stevie's shoulder. Big Steve knew that five or six bottles of water could get pretty heavy after ten or twelve minutes of carrying them over your shoulder. Little Stevie was short, but he was tough and he wasn't going to let his dad carry everything.

"Just as fine as frog's hair!" He answered back proudly. "I'm ready to put a line in the water, and pull out a whale!"

"That's the time!" Big Steve smiled and rubbed Little Stevie's thick, blonde hair. "But still, it's a twenty minute walk to the creek, so you let me know if that pack get's too heavy."

"I will."

Little Stevie was excited to be going fishing so he kept up a speedy pace and Big Steve had to move fast to keep up with his twelve year old son. In seventeen minutes they arrived at the creek bank and Little Stevie had barely broken a sweat.

"You got the worms Dad?" Little Stevie asked.

"You know it son. I got some big fat juicy ones too, so we oughta catch us a shark!"

"I'll settle for a big ol'e mud cat." Little Stevie said. "I wanna eat the *fish* Dad, I don't want the fish to eat *me*!"

"Good point son."

They got their hooks baited and sent the lines sailing through the air. Little Stevie and his Dad always giggled at the sounds that the sinkers made when they hit the water. Ploop! Ploop! This time was no different. They had their customary goofy laugh spell and then put on their game faces. It was time to catch some fish. Big Steve got the first nibble, but it was just a nibble. It was nothing to get hyper about. Then, Little Stevie felt the familiar tug on his line and saw the bending of the fiberglass rod.

He gave the rod a quick jerk up and back. "I got one Daddy, I got one!" Little Stevie tried to whisper but he was just too excited.

"Yea, me too son." Big Steve told him. "Just relax. Play him the way I showed you. Let him wear himself out a little before you try to reel him in."

"Okay Dad." Little Stevie replied with a calmer tone.

Little Stevie did exactly as his father had taught him. He pulled on the line a little, then he reeled in a little. He reeled it in, and let it out again, pulled in and let it out again. He let the fish think that it was in charge for a minute and it was fighting to stay in the water. Little Stevie was grunting and huffing and snorting like a mad baby bull every time the monster fish jumped and splashed and tried to tear himself free. "I got him Daddy! I got him!" Stevie yelled with excitement. "He's mine!" The fish was getting tired, but so was Little Stevie. He was a trooper though, and he finally pulled it in. It was a two pound bass. It might as well have been a whale. He had caught plenty of brim and catfish, but none of them had fought like that bass had. It was almost a foot long and it weighed two whole pounds!

An hour had passed and Stevie was ready to catch another one. He baited his hook and cast out to a shady area beneath the branches of a weeping willow. Big Steve had caught several fish already and Little Stevie wanted to catch just one more. He was reeling his line slowly, just trolling, when he saw his fishing rod bend like it never had before. "Daddy!" Little Stevie bellowed. "I got a big one!"

"Yea you do! Bring it in slowly son." He told Little Stevie. Big Steve fixed his eyes on the water where his son's line was. "That may not be a fish you've got there." He said calmly.

"What? What do you mean?" Little Stevie slowed his reeling down a bit. "What else could it be?"

"Just keep bringing him in slow, just like you're doing. We'll see what it is soon enough."

It looked like a huge dark ball was rising to the surface as Little Stevie continued pulling in his catch. As the shadowy figure broke the surface of the creek water however Big Steve knew that Little Stevie had caught a five foot cottonmouth. It was as thick as a tree limb and wadded itself up into a dark deadly ball around the bait. It was probably stuck on the fish hook too which had surely put it in a bad mood, and it just looked scary to Little Stevie. "Daddy!"

"Let it down Stevie! It's still on the hook! Just let it down!" Big Steve told his son, but he had already pulled it from the water and right about then the snake dropped to the ground, free from the fish hook that had snared him. The big water snake coiled itself up like it was preparing to strike.

"Don't move Stevie!" Said Big Steve. "I've got my pistol with me." Big Steve reached into the cargo pocket on the side of his pants and pulled out a .38 caliber pistol. He aimed it at the snake and pulled back the hammer.

"Wait Dad! Don't kill it!" Little Stevie wasn't as scared anymore. He picked up a tree branch that had recently fallen to the ground and scraped the leaves from it. The cottonmouth sensed a threat from the movement and reacted by moving slightly forward in a raised position, ready to bite if it had to. Little Stevie froze for a second, then realized that the snake stopped when he stopped.

"Be careful Stevie." Big Steve said with a whisper.

"It's okay Dad. I got this." Little Stevie took the stick by one end and began gently poking it in the snake's face to make it go away. The snake struck at the tree limb twice, reared up and began swaying back and forth. Little Stevie stuck the stick in the snake's face and for a minute it appeared as if the snake was just stubborn and wasn't going anywhere, anytime soon. Little Stevie then put the stick directly on the snake's nose and said, "You can go now, you snake in the grass! Go!" The snake continued to sway nervously, then it struck at the stick again. "Whoa there son!" Big Steve gasped. "It's okay dad. I promise." Little Stevie replied. He stood his ground, even when the snake lowered itself and moved a few inches in his direction. Little Stevie held the stick in the snake's face again and it stopped, like it was unsure of what to do. It coiled up again like it was going to strike, then slithered over to the bank, slid into the water and swam away. Big Steve was so impressed with his son's courage. "Little Stevie the snake charmer!" He praised his son. "That was something son! I'm proud of you! How did you know that would work?"

"I didn't. And I was ready to run just in case!" Little Stevie replied.

"I heard that!" Said Big Steve. "Well, how bout you and me head on home and see if we can't get your mother to cook up these here fish for supper?"

They had landed a total of eight fish big enough to eat. Three bass, three bream and two catfish. Little Stevie helped his dad clean the fish so mom could pan fry them later on that day. Little Stevie loved the way his mom cooked the fish, but it was only one o'clock in the afternoon and Big Steve was going to take a shower and then probably take a nap. He always took a nap after going fishing and Little Stevie always visited their neighbor Plowboy Jack.

***

Plowboy Jack was a farmer like a lot of folks in the community and was a good friend to Big Steve as well as Little Stevie. Little stevie had taken pictures of the fish and was going to show them to Plowboy Jack like he always did. Plowboy Jack liked it when Little Stevie visited him. It gave him an excuse to get down off his tractor for a few minutes. He was always on his tractor it seemed. His real name was Jackson Taylor and he had gotten the nickname Plowboy Jack one summer while working for another farmer many years ago as a teenager himself. He had caught a summer cold and passed it on to the farmer, rendering both of them unable to do any of the plowing that was scheduled to be done. Jackson had recovered sooner than the farmer had, and had begun the plowing while his boss lay in the bed with a fever. Jackson plowed for almost thirteen hours on the first day and then after only four hours of sleep he spent another ten hours on the tractor to finish what needed to be finished the next day. The word had spread about Jackson's twenty three hours on the seat of a tractor and one afternoon somebody yelled out to him as he passed by on a bicycle, "Hey, Plowboy Jack, git it boy!", and the name stuck.

"Hey Plowboy!" Little Stevie greeted his friend. "You ready to see some pictures of a couple of the biggest little bass ever catched out of Lowrun creek?"

"Catched?" Jack stuck out his hand and Little Stevie grabbed the huge paw.

"Yessir! Catched! I figured since we're such good friends I could relax a little bit and since I've always wanted to say it that way to somebody, catched it is!" He repeated. Little Stevie liked to mispronounce words and mix up the letters and say words backwards.

"You're going for your Phd next, right?" Jacked joked with him and patted him on the shoulder. "Let's see those photos!"

Little Stevie showed Plowboy Jack the pictures of the smaller ones first, and then he gave him the picture of the two pound bass that he had reeled in all by himself.

"Good giggly wiggly!" Plowboy Jack exclaimed. "You landed yourself a whale Little Stevie! Did you catch him all by yourself?"

"Yep. My dad was reeling in a monster himself and I had to fight that sucker all alone." Little Stevie bragged. "He weighed almost two pounds!"

"Wow!" Plowboy Jack said. "That's really something!"

"Thanks." Said Stevie. "We're gonna have him and his friends for supper later. Mom makes the best hushpuppies when Dad and I bring home fish to cook."

"Well, I hope they are as much fun to eat as they were to catch!"

"Me too!" Little Stevie said. "Hey! You wanna come over for dinner Plowboy? We've got plenty of fish!"

"I'd love to Stevie. But I've got to finish this field, and then I've got to burn some dead chickens."

"What?" Little Stevie asked. "What happened to your chickens?"

"A fox got in through a hole in the fence. Killed five or six hens and one rooster before I could get out here." Plowboy Jack started walking towards the chicken coop.

"A fox? Do you think he'll come back?" Stevie asked. "I've got a B.B. gun, and I'll keep my eyes open!"

"Well, you can't miss this one. He's mostly orange, with black feet and he's missing a big chunk out of his right ear." Jack said.

"I've already mended the fence but now I've got to get rid of the dead birds before other varmints get to sniffing around and causing problems."

"Can I see them before you burn them?"

"Well sure, if you really want to. Follow me." Jack said. He led Stevie around to the back of a shed where there were two big barrels that Plowboy Jack used to burn trash and other things.

"I'm gonna burn the dead birds in these barrels." Jack said. "If I don't, we'll have more critters around here than you can shake a stick at."

"How come?" Asked Little Stevie.

"Because animals like foxes and coyotes can smell blood and dead animals from miles away. Dead chickens can smell bad to us to us, but to a fox, they probably smell like a T-bone steak dinner." Plowboy Jack explained. "And a coyote would be licking his lips at the thought of a dead chicken for supper! The problem with that however, is if you leave the dead chickens out for the varmints to eat, they will keep coming around looking for handouts and sooner or later they will get around to eating your live chickens."

"Would the critters just dig them up if you buried them?" Little Stevie asked.

"Hey, you're getting wiser every day Stevie!" Plowboy Jack told him. "Yes, that's exactly what would happen." Jack put some small slivers of wood along with some small limbs into one of the barrels. He then tossed a few wadded up pieces of paper into the barrel and lit the last piece with a grill lighter. He used the last piece of paper to ignite the wadded up pieces of paper, then dropped it into the barrel.

Little Stevie stood back beside the pile of dead chickens and watched the blaze grow with every stick that Plowboy Jack dropped into the barrel. He stared, almost hypnotized by the glow, until his brain finally realized that his ears were trying to tell him something. He heard a sound almost like a rusty hinge on an old back porch screen door. Little Stevie looked around him and strained his ears to hear the sound again, but nothing. "Maybe I imagined it." Little Stevie told himself. But then he heard it again. He looked down beside him to his right. It wasn't a squeaky hinge, it was one of the chickens. But they were dead, or were they? Little Stevie knelt down in front of the big pile of feathers and began to look at all of the birds, one by one, to see if one of them might still be alive. All of them had their eyes open so it was hard to tell where the sound came from. Then Little Stevie saw the only rooster in the bunch and his eyes were moving. They moved just a little but it was enough. The rooster was still alive.

"Plowboy Jack!" Stevie yelled out. "The rooster's alive!"

Jack turned around and looked at Little Stevie. "What?"

"Yea, it's alive." Stevie told him. "Come see."

Jack walked over to where the chickens were. He looked down at the rooster with blood stained feathers and shook his head. "Humph!" He grunted. "Guess we need to put the poor thing out of it's misery." Jack walked into the barn and came out with an axe.

"What are you going to do?" Stevie asks.

"That rooster is just suffering Stevie. We need to go ahead and put him down."

"Can't you take him to a vet or something? Do you have to kill him?"

"I don't want to." Jack explained. "But I can't just take every chicken to the vet when they get almost eaten by a fox or some other predator. I'd spend a fortune on veterinarian bills if I did that. I'm sorry Stevie, but I just don't think that he would live anyway."

"Well, can I take him home with me? I mean, if you're going to… you know, put him down anyway."

Jack rubbed his chin. "Well, it would be alright with me, but what would your parents say about it?"

"I don't know." Stevie said thoughtfully. Then his eyes lit up. "I'll go talk to them right now, just don't do anything until I get back. Okay?" Little Stevie waited for Jack to answer. "Please!"

"Okay Stevie, you go talk to your mom and dad and I'll wait right here til you come back."

Little Stevie turned toward his house and walked. He picked up the pace then started a slow jog which turned into a trot and then a full sprint. Little Stevie yelled over his shoulder, "Don't do anything till I get back!"

"Okay!" Jack yelled after him. "I won't!" Plowboy Jack smiled and said to himself as he thought about how Little Stevie was going to talk his parents into this. "That crazy kid! I'd like to hear *that* conversation." He watched Little Stevie race uphill, through a field, around big rocks, over a ditch and through some briars to tell his parents about the half dead rooster that he wanted to bring home.

Less than ten minutes later Little Stevie came running back, huffing and puffing, and grinning from ear to ear.

"They said I could bring him home with me..." Stevie had to stop to catch his breath. "If it was okay with you!" He said.

"Okay Stevie, okay." Jack said. "You can have him, but you need to understand something. He might die anyway, and I don't want you to be too sad or disappointed if he does."

"I know." Stevie said. "But I'd like to try to save him."

"Well alright Stevie, let's wrap him up in a towel or something and you can take him home with you." Plowboy Jack started looking around for a small towel or some rags. "Wait right here Little Stevie, I'll be right back." Jack said and turned towards his barn. He stepped between the big doors and came back out a couple of minutes later with what looked like a basket and a huge white towel. "This ought to do nicely Little Stevie!" Jack said and grinned widely, showing a mouthful of good nature. He continued on toward the pile of dead chickens, minus one, and sat the basket down in front of the birds. He got out the towel, shook it out, and laid it back inside the basket, spread out and hanging out over the edges. "Now, let's wrap your rooster in this towel and let him rest in the basket while you carry him on home with you to Little Stevie's animal hospital."

"My rooster?" Little Stevie asked with fascination and began gently stroking the back of the injured rooster's head.

"Yes Little Stevie, your rooster. Now, do you think you can slide your hands under him, and lift him up?"

Little Stevie nodded. "I think so." He answered and turned his palms up. Then he dipped his hands down and moved them forward until the rooster rested on the palms of Little Stevie's hands. The rooster was a Rhode Island Red and it was hard to see the blood that was on him from his injuries. Little Stevie felt it however when he slid his hands under the rooster. It was warm and sticky but Little Stevie tried not to think about it too much.

"Be sure to keep one hand under his head and the other one under the biggest part of his body." Plowboy Jack instructed Little Stevie.

"Okay." Little Stevie said and lifted the rooster up. It made a sound like it was trying to crow, but it was just too weak and all that came out was the squeaking noise that it had made when Little Stevie first discovered it. Then the rooster surprised Little Stevie, and Plowboy Jack, by raising its head and pecking at

Little Stevie's hand. It made several efforts and finally got hold of Stevie's pinky finger. It held onto Little Stevie's knuckle skin, but it didn't hurt at all so Little Stevie just giggled and let the injured bird hang on with its beak. He laid the wounded rooster on the towel in the basket and it let go of Stevie's finger. The rooster then slowly laid its head down, with its eyes fixed on Little Stevie.

"What do you think his chances are?" Little Stevie asked Plowboy Jack. "I mean, do you think he's got any chance of living?"

"I don't know Stevie." Jack replied. "He's lost a good bit of blood, but I don't think he's bleeding any more." Little Stevie looked at the palms of his hands and they were covered in blood.

"I see what you mean." He said.

"Here, let's get your hands cleaned up before you go home and your mom has a hissy fit!" Jack laughed. He walked over to an outside spigot in front of the barn and turned on the water. "Come on Little Stevie, let's wash that blood off your hands!" Jack laughed again. Little Stevie gave the rooster a gentle stroke on his head and did as Jack had told him. The blood on his hands didn't really bother Little Stevie that much, he was just worried about *his* rooster. He washed his hands and dried them on the edge of the towel in the basket. He thanked Jack once again, picked up the basket with the rooster in it started for home.

"Oh, I almost forgot!" Jack said before Little Stevie got too far from the barn. "Hang on a second!" Jack disappeared into the barn again and came back out in a couple of minutes with several items in his hands. "Here, you're going to need these." He gave Little Stevie a tube of anti-bacterial cream, some Q-tip cotton swabs, some gauze pads and a small bottle of hydrogen peroxide.

"When you get him home, clean his wounds with the peroxide." Jack began. "You can dip the Q-tips into the peroxide or pour it onto the gauze pads. Then gently rub the swabs or the pads on his wounds until the peroxide starts bubbling. Then let it dry and put a tiny bit of this antibacterial cream on any open wounds you can see and if he survives the first couple of days, he just might make it."

"Do I need to put any bandages on him?" Little Stevie asked.

"No." Jack said. "I don't think you could get them to stay on his feathers anyway."

"Okay." Stevie said. "I'll let you know how he's doing in the morning before I go to school."

"I'll be waiting on ya!" Jack said.

Little Stevie picked up the basket and once again headed home.

"Aw, the poor thing." Stevie's mom said when she first saw the rooster. "Is he going to make it?" She asked and looked first at Little Stevie, and then at Big Steve.

"Sure!" Big Steve said. "He doesn't look hurt that bad to me."

"That's because you can't see all the blood because of his color." Little Stevie told his dad. "He's a Rhode Island Red and it's hard to see all the blood he lost. I had a lot of it on my hands until I washed it off, but Jack said that he wasn't bleeding anymore." Little Stevie reached into his pocket and pulled out the items that Plowboy Jack had given him as his mom tried not to scowl at the remark about all the blood on her son's hands.

"Plowboy Jack said I should clean out his wounds with this peroxide and these Q-tips, and then put some of this antibacterial cream on them."

"Yea, I guess so." Big Steve said. "Why don't we find him a comfortable spot over here by the fire place and do that right now."

Little Stevie carried the basket over to where Big Steve was and put it down on the floor. His mom brought over the peroxide and the Q-tips and handed them to Big Steve.

"Let me do it dad." Little Stevie said. "Plowboy Jack told me what to do."

"Okay Stevie. It's your rooster."

Little Stevie knelt down and began looking for the rooster's injuries. Once again the rooster pecked at Little Stevie and grabbed hold of a little piece of skin on the back of his hand. It still didn't hurt but mom had to look away. Little Stevie giggled again at the sensation and let out an "aha" when he located the first wound. The rooster still had Little Stevie's skin in his beak so Stevie moved that hand down to the towel and used his other hand to hold the rooster's head down while he got his finger loose. Big Steve dipped a Q-tip into the peroxide and gave it to his son. Little Stevie began softly rubbing the cotton swab back and forth on the wound and when he saw it bubbling he stopped rubbing and gently blew on the site. When it appeared dry he picked up the tube of anti-bacterial cream, unscrewed the cap and squeezed the tube until a tiny bit oozed out from the end. Big Steve gave him another cotton swab and Little Stevie put it into the ointment. Then he put the Q-tip to the wound site and spread it all over like peanut butter on bread. Little Stevie found three more places where the fox had bitten the rooster so he treated them in the same manner as he had the first one. He smoothed out all of the ruffled feathers, laid his rooster on the towel and pushed the basket against the wall.

"All we can do now is wait Stevie." Mom told him.

"No." Little Stevie said. "There's one more thing I can do!" Before mom could ask him what he was talking about he got down on his knees and said a little prayer for his rooster.

"Now we can wait, for him to get better! He's gonna make it!" Little Stevie said and got up off the floor.

***

Later that evening, around midnight, Little Stevie woke up and decided to check on the rooster. His mom had the same idea and the two of them ran into each other in the hallway.

"What are you doing up Stevie?" Mom asked. "It's after midnight, and you've got school tomorrow!"

"I know mom. But I couldn't sleep so I thought I would go check on H R."

"H R?" Mom asked.

"Yea." Little Stevie said. "That's what I named him. It's short for Hurt Rooster. Hey, what are *you* doing up?" Stevie asked.

"Uh, well, I wanted to check on H R too, oh, and look for your dad. He got up sometime while I was in the bathroom."

Little Stevie smiled. "Well, let's go check on him." He said. Mom opened the door to the den and there was Big Steve, squatted down in front of the basket talking to the rooster. He wasn't speaking loudly but mom and Little Stevie could hear him.

"Well honey, have you learned to speak *rooster-nese* and didn't tell me?" Mom asked and she and Little Stevie giggled together.

"Yea dad," Little Stevie said. "Did you ask him how he's feeling, or if he needs anything, like an aspirin or something."

"Ha ha." Big Steve smiled and then wrinkled his forehead. "Hey, you may have something there." He said. "He might just *be* in pain, and I've given aspirin and even tylenol to injured dogs before, and your rooster was wide awake when I came in here so let's give him a tiny piece of a baby aspirin and see if he doesn't rest a little better."

"Do you think it'll work?" Mom asked.

"I don't think it will hurt anything." Big Steve replied.

"Well, I'll go get one from the medicine cabinet." Mom said and turned toward the bathroom.

"Bring a couple of them." Big Steve said. "I just don't know how we're going to get him to swallow it."

"Yea, that might be a problem." Mom agreed with him and went to the medicine cabinet. She came back and Big Steve repeated himself. "How are we going to get him to swallow it?"

"I know!" Little Stevie cried out. "Let me have it dad!"

"What are you gonna do Stevie?"

" I've got an idea. Every time I put my hand near his beak he pecks one of my fingers and holds on, so maybe we can wet the piece of aspirin and stick it to the back of my hand. Then I'll stick my hand up to his beak and when he grabs hold of my hand, I can tilt it and maybe the aspirin will go down his throat."

"Hey, that's a great idea Stevie." Big Steve praised his son. "It just might work!"

Mom went and got a bottle of water from the kitchen and gave it to her husband. Big Steve dipped his finger into the bottle and got a drop of water on the tip of his index finger, then put a small piece of the baby aspirin into the water. "Gimme your hand Stevie."

Little Stevie put out his right hand and Big Steve carefully put the piece of aspirin on the back of it.

"Yea, right there dad." Little Stevie said. "That'll work." Little Stevie put his hand up close to the rooster's beak and began talking to him. "There you go H R, this is gonna make you feel a lot better." The rooster began making those noises that roosters make, like the sound of a squeaky door hinge and Little Stevie knew that the rooster was about to peck his hand. "Get ready for it." He said and as soon as he got the words out of his mouth, the rooster struck. He pecked Little Stevie's hand below the knuckle where the aspirin was and held on. Little Stevie put his left hand behind the rooster's head and tilted his right hand to the left. He saw the aspirin slide off of his hand and down the rooster's throat. The rooster then had to turn loose of Little Stevie's hand to completely swallow the little bit of aspirin. He raised his head the way roosters do when they're getting ready to swallow something, started jiggling his throat muscles and the aspirin disappeared down his throat.

"That, is how you do that!" Little Stevie said proudly and Big Steve rubbed his head.

"That was a good idea son."

"Thanks dad."

In a few minutes the rooster actually seemed to be resting so mom suggested that they all go back to bed. "Six thirty is going to be here in no time guys!" Mom told them. "Let's hit the sack!"

"Good idea!" Both Big Steve and Little Stevie said at the same time and laughed.

"Nice!" Little Stevie said.

They all went to bed and got some well needed rest, and H R the rooster even seemed to be resting peacefully. Little Stevie was the first one up that morning and the first thing he did was check on his rooster. As Little Stevie entered the living room the rooster did what roosters do early in the morning. It crowed, and it crowed, and it crowed. It was still a bit weak, but Little Stevie was thrilled about it anyway. He knew it was a sign that his rooster was going to be okay and he was so excited about it that he ran into his parents bedroom to tell them the news. "Mom, Dad!" He yelled as he opened their door. "Did you hear him? Did you hear H R crow?" Little Stevie asked. Big Steve and mom were awake, but just hadn't gotten out of bed yet.

"Yes son, we heard him." Big Steve grumbled sleepily, still rubbing his eyes. "How in the world could we not hear him?"

"Uh, yea, I guess." Little Stevie said. "I told you he was gonna be alright!"

"I know son. And you are probably right, but that's what roosters do in the morning so just don't get your hopes too high. He's still got some healing to do." Big Steve reminded him.

"I know dad, but you just gotta believe. You gotta think positive!"

"Well, you've got that covered Stevie!" Mom said. "Now let's get breakfast going before you men get out of here."

"Okay mom." Little Stevie said. "What do you think we should feed H R?"

"Well if he doesn't like your mom's biscuits, he's got some brain damage, and there's no cure for *that*!" Big Steve joked.

"Yea, chickens are not usually picky when it comes to food." Mom said. "We'll give him some of a biscuit when I get them done, okay?"

"Okay, I'll go get ready for school."

"Yea, and I've got to get ready to go to work." Big Steve said and got out of the bed.

After breakfast Little Stevie crumbled up a piece of a biscuit and put in in a small bowl. He took it into the living room and to his surprise the rooster was standing in the basket. It flapped its wings when Little Stevie came into the room like it was showing off for him. Then it crowed again and stretched its neck. Little Stevie set the bowl in front of H R and the rooster gobbled up the bread in no time. Then it began looking around for more to eat so Little Stevie hollered for his mom to bring him another biscuit. "H R seems to be really hungry this morning!" He said as mom brought in another buttermilk delight. Little Stevie crumbled it up like before and just like before, the rooster made it disappear.

"Wow!" Mom said. "He really *was* hungry!"

"I told you. He's gonna be alright!" Stevie said proudly.

Big Steve came into the room. "Did he eat anything?" He asked.

"Did he eat anything?" Mom echoed Big Steve. "I'll say he did. He devoured a biscuit and a half in about thirty seconds!"

"Hey, who does that remind you of?" Big Steve put Little Stevie in a headlock and rubbed his head. Then he kissed his son on the head and gave it another good rub. "Little Man here eats his share, that's for sure!"

"I'm a growing boy Dad." Little Stevie said.

"Son, I'm not sure, but you might have shrunk half an inch or so in the last year."

"Steve!" Mom exclaimed. "You're gonna give the boy a complex!"

"What?" Big Steve asked.

"No, that's okay mom! He can keep it!" Little Stevie joked. "I don't want one." He said. "Uh, what's a complex?"

"It's like when somebody doesn't like themselves very much son." Big Steve explained. "Like when they don't think that they're worth anything."

"Yes, and it usually comes from a kid's parents saying bad things about him or her and making them feel bad about themselves." Mom butted in.

"But I didn't..." Big Steve began.

"Well, why was Dad gonna give me one of those?" Little Stevie interrupted and slapped his knee at the joke he had made.

"I was just making a joke honey!" Big Steve told his wife.

"It's okay Dad. It doesn't bother me." Said Little Stevie. "Besides, I'm one of my favorite people, and I *love* all my favorite people!"

"Ya see?" Big Steve said. "Little Stevie got it. The joke I mean!"

"Oh no! No no!" Mom fired back jokingly. "Don't try to apologize now."

"Is that what I was doing?" Big Steve asked. "Apologizing?"

Little Stevie butted in. "Dad, why don't you quit while you're, uh, not so far behind."

"That's probably a good idea son. I think I will."

Big Steve reached over and kissed his wife on the cheek. "You win honey." He said.

"As usual!" She boasted. "Now I'm going to clean up the kitchen while you fellas finish getting ready. We're leaving in twenty minutes Stevie."

"Okay mom, I'll be ready."

Nineteen minutes later Mom pulled out of the driveway with Little Stevie in the passenger seat. He asked his mom to stop at Plowboy Jack's so Little Stevie could tell Jack the good news about the rooster. Big Steve had left only a couple of minutes earlier and it looked like it was going to be a fine day. Mom arrived at school half an hour early and Little Stevie saw Donald through the cafeteria window. He was at their usual table with the usual friends and they seemed to be having a lively conversation. Donald was waving his arms around in an excited manner like he was explaining the fine details of advanced orangutan warfare. Little Stevie also noticed that the table behind their usual table, where the bullies sat, was totally empty. "Hmm." He said to himself wishfully. "Maybe they were all put into a round room and were told to go sit in the corner. They'll be gone forever!" Little Stevie snickered.

"Have a great day Stevie!" Mom said as he shut the door.

"Bye mom!"

***

Mom pulled off and Little Stevie entered the cafeteria to greetings from the table. "Little Stevie!" Three of his group said at almost the same time.

"So, what's up with the genius table?" Little Stevie asked and pointed with his thumb over his shoulder. "They get lost on the way to the bus stop?"

"Nah." Donald replied. "I think somebody said their bus had a flat, and they're going to be late."

"That's too bad." Said Little Stevie. "I miss them so much this morning!" He laughed and sat down beside Donald.

"Hey man." Said Donald. "I heard something you might want to know about."

"What?" Asked Little Stevie.

"I'll tell you on the way to homeroom."

"Okay man." Little Stevie said.

"Hey, I wonder if Barney and the bullies had anything to do with the flat tire on the bus." One of the group said and they all laughed. "That's funny." Someone else added. "But it could be true."

They all stopped laughing at once, each looking around the table to see the others reactions, then burst out with laughter again and they all agreed that it could be possible. After a couple of minutes the topic of conversation changed. First to one middle school thing, then another and before long it was time to go to homeroom.

Little Stevie and Donald had been in the same homeroom from the first grade on up and since they were almost next door neighbors, it was natural that they were best friends. On their way to homeroom Donald and Little Stevie both had to go to the restroom. There was nobody else in there so Little Stevie asked Donald what it was that he had heard. "So, you gonna tell me what you heard that I might want to know about?" Little Stevie asked while they were both washing their hands.

"Oh yea. Do you remember my cousin Adonia that lives in Springdale?"

"Yea, I think so." Little Stevie replied. "Is she the cute one with the long black hair?"

"Yea, that's her." Donald said and pulled some paper towels out of the dispenser to dry his hands.

"What about her? What did she say?"

"Well, she's got this friend that is *Barney's* cousin, and she overheard Barney say something on the phone about busting somebody up for getting him and his friends in trouble at school."

"Really?" Little Stevie asked. "I guess that would be me."

"Yea, I guess it would." Donald said. "But she also said that Barney's cousin said that they were going to try and catch whoever it was, away from school, so all you have to do is avoid running into Barney or any of his buddies when you're not at school."

"Well, that ought to be easy enough." Said Little Stevie. "As long as I stay at *home* forever!" He added. "Man, it's so tough being me!"

"Yea, it is kind of a small town." Donald agreed.

"Tell me about it man. I think we're the only town in America with half a zip code."

"Seriously dude?" Donald asked.

"Uh, no. I was kidding." Replied Little Stevie. "It's just that everybody knows everybody here, and you don't have to go very far to go anyplace that's anywhere in this place. Do you know what I mean?"

"Yea, I get it. It's a small town. Whatcha gonna do?"

"Get a guard dog!"

"Really Stevie?"

"No, I was kidding again. But it wouldn't be a bad idea ya know." Little Stevie paused as the two of them exited the restroom and started toward homeroom. "Yea, I'd love to have a great big

Doberman pinscher, that I could sic on Barney and his buddies anytime they came near me."

"Yea!" Said Donald. "I'd give anything to be able to watch them all cry like a bunch of little girls while a guard dog tore the rears out of their breeches!"

"Yea." Echoed Little Stevie. "Hey, did I tell you I've got a pet rooster now?"

"Naw man. Where d'you get a pet rooster?"

"Plowboy Jack." Little Stevie replied. "A fox got into his hen house, killed a bunch of chickens and one rooster, almost."

"Oh yea? Almost?"

"Yea man, he had the dead chickens in a pile, because he was going to burn them, and I heard a sound like a squeaky hinge and it turned out to be this rooster up under a couple of the dead hens."

"And it was still alive?" Asked Donald.

"Yea, but barely." Said Little Stevie. "The poor thing was hurt pretty bad. Well, still is, but he's getting better every day."

"And Plowboy Jack just gave it to you?"

"Well yea." Replied Little Stevie. "I mean, Jack didn't think it would live anyway, so yea, he just gave me the rooster."

"Humph!" Snorted Donald. "So, what do you do with a pet rooster?"

"Well haven't *you* ever had a pet rooster?" Asked Little Stevie with a sly grin on his face.

"Well sure, who hasn't?" Exclaimed Donald. "No, I never had a pet rooster."

"Me either, and I've seen dead chickens before, but for some reason I wanted to see if I could save this one. Ya know?"

"Yea." Donald said, then shook his head. "Hey, when have you ever seen dead chickens?"

"At the dinner table!" Laughed Little Stevie. "The ones that my mom cooks in the deep fryer aren't exactly clucking and scratching around on the kitchen floor!"

"Well, aren't you a riot today!" Said Donald. "Mr Funny man!"

"Nah, I was just messing with you." Said Little Stevie. "I've seen a couple of dead chickens over at Plowboy Jack's place before. Never up close though, just from a distance when my Dad and I were over there."

"Yea, I guess so." Said Donald. "It *is* a farm, and I guess that chickens die from time to time on a farm."

"Of course they do!" Little Stevie agreed. "But it just wasn't his time and now I've got a pet rooster! After all, I couldn't just let it die."

"Yea." Said Donald. "Sometimes you just know something's right, and you do it."

"Exactly!" Said Little Stevie. "And Mom and Dad saw it that way too, and now I've got a pet rooster!"

"And you don't know what you're gonna do with it?"

"Well, first of all I've got to see that he gets one hundred per-cent better." Little Stevie said. "And then I'll figure out what you do with a pet rooster!"

"Sounds good!" Said Donald.

***

Later that afternoon while waiting with the car riders, Little Stevie invited Donald over to see his pet rooster. "Yea, he's almost well enough for us to put him outside in the pen that my Dad built." Little Stevie told Donald while they were waiting for their rides.

"Did he make it fox proof?" Donald asked.

"Oh yea!" Said Little Stevie. "I don't think a bear could get into *that* pen!"

"No need to worry about a fox then, huh?"

"No, unless it was a fox as big as an elephant!" Little Stevie replied.

"That's good." Donald said. "Hey, my mom's here! I'll be over around five. Okay?"

"I'll be there dude."

A few minutes later Little Stevie's mom arrived to pick him up and when they got home Stevie went right in to check on his rooster. Stevie's dad had moved the rooster into the garage the day before because it was able to walk around fairly well and that meant it would be getting messy in the house. Little Stevie had taken great care of the rooster by keeping down infections with peroxide and antibacterial cream. He also spoon fed the rooster until it was able to eat on it's own and he even gave him pieces of baby aspirin for the first few days to make sure that the rooster was as pain free as possible.

Donald and his mom arrived at five o'clock and Little Stevie's mom invited her in for coffee.

"You know that you're going to have to clean up any mess the rooster makes, right?" Mom told Little Stevie as he and Donald started out the front door to go into the garage. "Oh, and any mess that he's already made."

"How much of a mess can one rooster make, mom?" Little Stevie asked.

"Well, roosters go to the potty just like everybody else Stevie." She replied. "And yours has been going, and going, and going, all day long. You'll see when you get out there!"

"Okay mom. I'll take care of it."

"And Donald will help you Stevie." Donald's mom said. "Won't you son?"

"Yes ma'am!"

Little Stevie and Donald entered the garage through the side door and they saw what Stevie's mom was talking about.

"Holy crap!" Little Stevie exclaimed.

"Well, I don't know how holy it is." Said Donald. "But it *is* crap! And a lot of it!"

"Yea, and we gotta clean it up!" Said Little Stevie.

"Who's we?" Asked Donald. "You got a frog in your pocket or something?"

"Okay, *I've* got to clean it up!" Said Little Stevie.

"I'm just kiddin man. I'll help you out."

"I knew you would." Little Stevie said. "And your mom knew it too. I guess we'd better hurry up and get the *crap* outta here. Ha ha. Get it?"

"What?" Asked Donald. "Oh, yea I get it. You *are* gonna use gloves aren't you Mr funny man?"

"No, *we're* gonna use gloves though."

"You know what I mean Stevie."

"Yea well, let's go get some and get started. We're gonna need a couple of brooms, a dustpan and a shovel too I guess."

"Yea, and a water hose wouldn't hurt either." Said Donald.

"Hey, that's a great idea Donald! We can sweep it all up into a pile over by the big doors and then just turn the water on it and wash it out into the ditch by the driveway!"

"Yea?" Donald said with a little bit of a question in his voice. "That *was* a good idea of mine wasn't it?" He added.

"Yes it was! I knew there was a good reason we were friends!" Little Stevie joked.

Little Stevie put the rooster in a small cage that he had borrowed from Plowboy Jack to keep him from getting too excited and hurting himself. He and Donald then put on some old work gloves of Big Steve's and began sweeping the chicken poop over toward the big garage doors. A lot of it had dried and that made it a little easier to sweep. After they had swept up all that they could, Little Stevie brought in the water hose. Donald turned on the water and Little Stevie aimed the nozzle at the pile of dried chicken manure. In only a couple of minutes the water washed it all into the ditch beside the driveway. Then he let Donald take over with the nozzle to clean the inside of the garage that was stained with the rooster droppings. In no time at all the garage floor was spic and span and all they had to do then was dry things up a little bit and the job was done. The rooster meanwhile paced back and forth in the cage, stopping a few times to gaze at the stream of water and to show his disapproval with some wing flapping. When they were finished Little Stevie closed the garage doors and let the rooster out of the cage.

"I think he'll be able to stay in his pen before too long." Little Stevie told Donald as he stroked the back of the rooster's head.

"I never saw a chicken let somebody pet it like that." Donald said. "You know, like a dog or a cat."

"Yea I know." Little Stevie replied. "It's like he knows I'm not gonna hurt him, or maybe he just likes it. I don't know."

"And you *did* save his life. I mean, he would be a pile of ashes right now if it wasn't for you."

"Yea, I guess so." Little Stevie said and stopped petting the rooster to scratch his own head. The rooster began flapping his wings again, only this time it was to fly. It didn't fly away however, it went up and came down, landing on Little Stevie's arm. Little Stevie and Donald looked at each other in awe for a second, then stared at the rooster to see what it was going to do next. The rooster flapped it's wings yet again and crowed loudly, clutching Little Stevie's arm with his talons. It didn't hurt so Little Stevie didn't mind and the rooster jumped off his arm quickly enough. Then he crowed once more before going back into the cage. The rooster simply stared at them both as if to say, "Okay, I'm going to rest now, so you can leave." Little Stevie and Donald were amazed at the rooster's behavior. They closed the cage and went inside to tell mom about it.

"Did you guys get all that mess cleaned up?" She asked.

"Yes we did mom!" Little Stevie replied excitedly. "But you're not going to believe what H R did!"

"H R? You mean the rooster?" She glanced over at Donald's mom and smiled. "Hurt rooster." She said.

"Yes ma'am!" Little Stevie answered. "Me and Donald were out in the garage and…"

"Me and Donald? Don't you mean Donald and I?"

"Yes ma'am. Donald and I." Little Stevie corrected himself. "We were out in the garage checking on the rooster and he started flapping his wings like he was going to fly off somewhere, and then he flew up and landed on my arm!"

"What?" Mom asked.

"Yes ma'am. Then he jumped off my arm, hit the floor and went back into his cage and just sat there and stared at us until we left."

"Really?"

"Yes ma'am. It was like he wanted us to leave so he could rest or something!"

"It was really cool!" Said Donald. "And Little Stevie pets him like a dog or a cat and the rooster lets him!"

"Wow!" Said Mom. "That *is* pretty cool."

"Yea!" Said Little Stevie. "He must be the smartest rooster in the world! I'll bet I can even teach him some tricks like a dog or something!"

"Yea!" Echoed Donald. "Like an attack dog! And then you could sic him on Barney and those other knuckleheads!"

They all turned their heads at the sound of a car in the driveway and Little Stevie ran toward the front door. "It's dad! I gotta tell him all about it! Come on Donald, let's go!"

Little Stevie and Donald both sprang out the front door and met Big Steve as he was getting out of his pick-up truck. Little Stevie then told his dad the whole story exactly as he had told it to his mom. He told him about the rooster flying up and landing on his arm and how *that* was a good sign that the rooster was getting better. Then he told Big Steve about the rooster's odd behavior when it went back into the cage on it's own and how they would probably be able to put H R out in his pen soon.

"It's a coop." Said Donald.

"What?" Little Stevie asked with a puzzled look on his face.

"Donald's right Stevie." Said Big Steve. "It's called a chicken coop, not a pen."

"Oh, okay." Replied Little Stevie. "Well, pretty soon H R can go out into his chicken coop and we won't have to clean up any more chicken poop!"

Big Steve and Donald both laughed at the rhyme that Little Stevie had made, and then Little Stevie realized what he had done and he laughed as well.

"That was a good one son! Is supper ready? I'm starving!"

"I don't know dad."

"Something smells good!" Donald said as they opened the door and went inside.

"Yes it does Donald. You gonna stick around and eat with us?" Big Steve asked.

"No, I've got supper cooking at home too!" Donald's mom answered before he could.

"Aw mom, can't we just…" Donald began.

"No, we can't just anything." She said and gave Little Stevie a wink. "Your dad is probably home by now too!" Then she looked at Big Steve. "We just came over to see Little Stevie's pet rooster and sit with your lovely wife and enjoy a cup of coffee."

"Well, y'all are welcome to stay and eat with us any time."

"Oh, I know that Steve. Thank you for asking." Donald's mom said. "But we've got to get on home. Let's go son, I've got your favorite, keeping warm in the oven. It's your dad's favorite too, so we had better get going if you want to eat tonight!"

"Okay mom." Donald said. "I'll see you tomorrow Stevie."

"Bye y'all!" Donald's mom waved as she and her son left.

***

"She's a sweet gal." Big Steve said about Donald's mom as he watched them pull out of the driveway. "How long before supper's ready honey?"

"Oh, half an hour or so I suppose." Little Stevie's mom replied. "Why, you got a date or something?"

"Yea, but that's not until after supper...with you!" Big Steve grabbed her around the waist and gave her a peck on the cheek. "No, I thought Little Stevie and I would get in a little boxing practice if we had the time, and it looks like we do!"

"Oh yea!" Little Stevie shouted and began shadow boxing. Then he raised his hands above his head and quoted a heavyweight champion from the past. "I am the greatest!" Then he threw a few punches in his dad's direction. "Put'em up! Put'em up!" He said while his mom looked on with a motherly smile on her face.

"Okay Rocky." She said. "Just don't get too sweaty or dirty when you and Smokey Joe wear eachother out."

"We won't honey." Said Big Steve. "And it's *Smoking* Joe, not Smokey Joe. As in Smoking Joe Frazier! You know, the former heavyweight champion of the world!"

"Well, how could he be champion of anything if he was a smoker?" Mom wanted to know.

"Naw! He wasn't a smoker!" Big Steve said. "That was just a nickname!"

"Why on earth would he have a nickname like that if he didn't smoke? I didn't think athletes were supposed to smoke."

"Not that kind of smoking Honey." Big Steve went on. "It's kind of like when you take off in a car and you squall your tires and smoke comes out, or when something gets so hot that it smokes, or, well you get it. Right?"

"No." She said.

Big Steve scratched his head. "Well, it's like, uh, well…"

"Explain it to me later dear." Mom cut him off. "I've got to set the table and check on the meatloaf if you guys are hungry. So just get on with your rough housing and teach my baby how to be a brute, but remember, don't get too sweaty and all nasty!" She winked at Little Stevie and turned away.

Big Steve had set up a small workout area in the garage and Little Stevie began skipping rope rope to warm up. Big Steve told Little Stevie to always warm up before doing any type of physical exercise and he said that skipping rope was one of the best ways to warm up. Big Steve had also said that it was a great way to build up stamina in his legs as well as his lungs.

"A lot of times, if you can outlast your opponent, you can beat him." Big Steve had told him many times since they had started training. "Most street fights only last a few seconds." He told Little Stevie. "Because one or both of them usually get tired, and when that happens, folks start to wonder what the fight was all about to begin with."

Little Stevie skipped rope for three, two minute rounds while the rooster watched from inside the cage. At the end of every round the bell on the timer would sound and Little Stevie would stop. The rooster made a fuss every time Little Stevie stopped skipping rope as if he was cheering him on so Little Stevie raised his hands in victory every time as well.

Big Steve then showed him how to put on the hand wraps, like he had done before. "You have to do it a bunch of times before you get the hang of it son." He said when Little Stevie seemed to be getting frustrated. "But they are very important, so you don't hurt your hands when you hit the punching bag."

After Big Steve made sure that the handwraps were on right, he and Little Stevie walked over to the heavy bag. It was a canvas type punching bag filled with sand and it weighed around fifty pounds. Big Steve put a pair of training gloves on Little Stevie's hands and told him to start out slow and easy, getting the feel of it before throwing harder and faster punches. He started Little Stevie out with a few left jabs, one at a time, then putting two and three punches together for "combination" punching. "When you land one punch," Big Steve said. "Your opponent is at least off balance, so always follow up with one or two more shots."

Little Stevie was doing just like his dad instructed him, and was beginning to show some real progress. The rooster seemed to think so as well. Every time Little Stevie threw only one punch, the rooster barely made a sound. Every time Little Stevie threw a two, three, or four punch combination however, the rooster cackled and flapped his wings in approval.

On that particular day Big Steve had decided that it was time to let his son feel what a punch to the face or head felt like, in case he ever had to actually defend himself. Big Steve hoped it would never come to that, but he wanted Little Stevie to be ready for it, if that day ever came. Little Stevie took off the gloves he had used for hitting the heavy bag, and he and Big Steve both put on a pair of sixteen ounce sparring gloves. Sparring is when two people actually practice boxing and they use "sparring gloves".

Big Steve got down on his knees and once again he told Little Stevie to take it slow at first, to ease into it. He let Little Stevie strike first by sticking his head out and telling Little Stevie to punch him on the forehead. After taking a couple of shots to the head from his son, Big Steve began tapping Little Stevie lightly on *his* forehead. It didn't hurt at all so Little Stevie shouted out, "Harder ya big sissy! Mom hits harder than that!"

Big Steve laughed at his son, and then wound up his arm like he was going to give him a good solid shot to the face. As soon as he started to throw the fake punch however, the rooster cackled and screeched and began flapping his wings wildly. Then he started slamming himself against the inside of the cage until Little Stevie thought that the rooster was going to hurt himself all over again.

"Whoa boy! Whoa!" Little Stevie said as he rushed over to the cage and pulled off the boxing gloves. "It's okay now. We're done."

Big Steve walked up to the cage as well and the rooster screeched and flapped his wings again until Big Steve backed up a couple of steps.

"Wow!" Big Steve said. "What got into him? He acted like I was going to hurt you and he was gonna have your back!"

"Yea I know." Little Stevie replied.

Big Steve stepped a little closer and the rooster made a fuss again. He stepped back and thought for a second. "Let me try something." Big Steve said and stepped around Little Stevie. He walked around to the other side of the cage and stood there for a few seconds. The rooster ignored him and focused on Little

Stevie, so Big Steve knelt down and put his hand up to the cage. The rooster remained calm and still so Big Steve stood up and went back around to where his son was. He made a fist and faked a slow punch in Little Stevie's direction. The rooster went wild again with his wings flapping so Big Steve backed off again.

"I think you've made yourself a friend for life there son!" Big Steve laughed. "You saved his life and I think he knows it, somehow. And even if he doesn't, he has taken a liking to you for *some* reason."

"Yea." Said Little Stevie "It's kinda weird, you know. He acts like a guard dog that's been trained to protect me, and when he thought you were going to hit me, he just went nuts!"

"That's exactly what he did. He went nuts, and was doing his best to get out of that cage and come after *me*!"

"Yea, just like a guard dog!" Little Stevie repeated.

"You know what son?" Big Steve asked. "You may have the world's first, *guard rooster*!"

"I think you're right dad. You know, he lets me pet him like a dog too." Little Stevie said.

"He does?"

"Yessir!" Replied Little Stevie. "And he even eats out of my hand."

"Wow." Said Big Steve. "That's really something! Did you teach him any of that?"

"No sir. He started doing it all on his own."

"Well, he sure enough didn't like it when he thought I was going to hit you." Said Big Steve. "In fact, I'll bet that he would have spurred me something good if he could have gotten out of that cage!"

"Spurred you?" Asked Little Stevie. "What's that?"

"Look right there, at his feet." Big Steve pointed at the rooster's spurs. "Do you see those things on on both of his ankles, just above his feet?"

"Yessir." Answered Little Stevie.

"Well, those are called spurs. And that's what roosters use to defend themselves." Big Steve told Little Stevie. "And they can do *some kind* of damage if they get a hold of you with those things!"

"Really?" Asked Little Stevie.

"Yea. I've gone to a couple of cock fights, a long time ago, and most of the time one of the roosters end up killing the other one with their spurs."

"A cock fight? What's that?"

"That's when they put two roosters, that are trained to fight, into a small circle and let them go at it." Little Stevie's forehead wrinkled up as Big Steve told him about cock fighting. "People like to bet money on which one they think will win and so that's one of the main reasons they have cock fights."

"That's just mean." Said Little Stevie. "It oughta be against the law!"

"Oh, it *is* against the law in most places." Said Big Steve. "But people still do it."

"Humph!" Snorted Little Stevie. "Well, my rooster's not ever gonna do anything like that!"

"I hope not." Big Steve said. "Cause like I said, most of the time one of the roosters dies."

"Humph!" Little Stevie repeated.

Mom called them in for supper so Little Stevie made sure that the rooster was secure in his cage while Big Steve checked the big roll up door and the small side door to the garage. Little Stevie told Big Steve that he was going to give the rooster his food and water after supper so they closed the doors and went inside to eat.

"Mmm! It smells de-*lish*!" Big Steve bragged and licked his lips. He and Little Stevie sat down as mom took the meatloaf out of the oven. She brought it to the table and Little Stevie already had his fork in his hand ready to dig in. Mom set the hearty dish on the table and turned to go and get the rest of supper. She had prepared green beans and macaroni with cheese, along with some of her famous jalapeno cornbread that Little Stevie liked so much. When she returned to the table both Little Stevie and his dad were picking at the meatloaf with their forks. Mom set the cornbread down and lightly slapped both of them on the hands. "Aren't y'all forgetting something?"

"Yes ma'am!" They said at the same time and bowed their heads. Little Stevie gave thanks and Big Steve said "Amen". Then they both dug in and ate until they were fat and happy and couldn't move. Then they sat on the couch and turned on the TV. Reruns of The Andy Griffith show were on and it was one of their favorites. Little Stevie liked to make fun of Barney's big, bug eyes and Big Steve liked Floyd the barber. Mom could hear them laughing from the kitchen and it warmed her heart to know that her Big man and her Little man were so close and could share something so simple as an old TV show and get so much enjoyment from it.

After she was done cleaning up the kitchen Mom joined her two men and they watched Jeopardy. Little Stevie was always up for a challenge when it came to trivia and Big Steve had once played Trivial Pursuit with some college friends for eleven hours. Mom had a fairly good memory as well when it came to trivia so along with being really fun to watch, Jeopardy provided mental exercise for the entire family.

"What was The Treaty of Versailles?" Mom asked in response to the answer that Alex Trebek gave on their TV screen.

Big Steve and Little Stevie both just stared at her in shock when the participant on Jeopardy gave the same answer and Alex said it was correct. Mom raised her hands in victory. "I am the greatest!" She shouted in imitation of her son. "Git sum!" She added as Big Steve turned down the volume on the television set.

"Wow!" Big Steve said to his wife. "You're smarter than I thought you were."

"What are you saying Dad? That Mom's not smart?" Little Stevie asked.

"Uh, isn't it your bedtime son?" Big Steve replied. "Or don't you have a rooster to feed or something?"

"Yea Dad, are you saying that I'm not smart?" Asked Mom jokingly.

"Oh no honey! No, no, no!" Big Steve blurted out defensively. "You uh, uh…"

"Did *you* know the question to the answer that Alex gave?" Mom asked him.

"Well, no!" Big Steve confessed. "But…"

"Enough said then!" Mom turned and walked away as proud as a peacock.

Big Steve turned around and Little Stevie was staring at him with one eyebrow raised.

"Well, you didn't know the answer either!" Big Steve said with a slightly embarrassed grin on his face.

"Actually Dad, I did." Replied Little Stevie. "It was the question that I didn't know."

"Aw, you know what I mean!" Big Steve laughed and told Little Stevie to go and feed his chicken.

"It's a rooster Dad. And I'm going, I'm going."

H R the rooster already had some food in his feeder, Little Stevie made sure that he had enough water and just sat out by the cage for a while. After a few minutes Little Stevie opened the door to the cage to let H R walk around for a bit, but instead the rooster stayed right by Little Stevie's side. Little Stevie figured that the rooster needed some exercise so he began walking around the garage. At first Little Stevie just walked at a normal pace but then he picked up his step a little bit. The faster Little Stevie walked, the faster the rooster walked. Whenever Stevie stopped, the rooster stopped. Little Stevie knelt down to get a look at the rooster's wounds and he could barely see them then. He was healing up nicely Little Stevie thought and soon, maybe tomorrow, he and Big Steve would transfer the rooster to his newly constructed home just outside the garage. The only thing that worried Little Stevie was the idea of the fox coming back and finishing what he had started, even though his dad had told him that there was no way that a fox could get into that coop.

Little Stevie yawned and the rooster stared at him, cocking his head from side to side. Little Stevie thought about something and shook the yawn off. Then he stuck his right arm out in front of him and waited. The rooster paced back and forth twice, then flapped his wings and crowed. He flapped his wings again, but this time it was to fly. Just like before he flew up a few feet and landed on Little Stevie's arm. "That's just what I thought you would do!" Little Stevie said. He reached up and rubbed the rooster's head and the back of his neck before he squatted down to put the rooster away for the night.

"Alright buddy, it's time to get a little shuteye." Little Stevie said to the rooster as he held his arm in front of the door to the cage. The rooster jumped off of his arm and he waved him in like a base runner. "There you go, nice and snug, and safe in here!" The rooster obeyed Little Stevie's every command like a well trained dog. He went right into the cage, stopped and turned around like he was waiting for the next order. Little Stevie closed the cage and latched it as the rooster flapped it's wings and crowed again. "See ya bright and early buddy!" Little Stevie went inside and got ready for bed. "Goodnight little man." Mom said and kissed him on the forehead after he laid down. "Goodnight Stevie!" Big Steve called from the doorway.

"Goodnight mom, goodnight dad!"

The next morning Little Stevie's mom carried him to school, as usual, and as usual his friends were waiting for him at their usual table. Donald had told them all about Stevie's rooster so by the time Little Stevie arrived, they wanted to hear more about him.

"What color is it? How big is he? What do you do with a rooster? Did you really save his life?" Those were some of the questions that Little Stevie was bombarded with when he arrived at school. Little Stevie patiently answered everyone's questions and as he was sitting down at the table with his friends, a final question was asked from behind him.

"I wonder if he's gonna taste better fried or barbecued?" It was Barney. Little Stevie got scared at first, but then he got mad! He spun around on the seat and stood up to face Barney. It wasn't only Barney however, there were three of his bully buddies along side of him. Little Stevie had several friends there with him as well but Donald was the only one that stood up with him.

"I guess we're never gonna find out, *Barney*!" Little Stevie exclaimed loudly. He was getting tired of Barney and his buddies picking on him and anybody else they wanted to, simply because they were bigger than everybody else. "Cause you're not ever going to put your hands on him!"

"Oh yea?" Barney fired back. "What are you gonna do about it?"

Little Stevie wanted to just punch Barney in the nose, but he knew that he would probably get the tar whipped out of him, right then. "Now is not the time." He thought to himself. "A few more weeks though, and I'll be good enough to rope a dope the fire out of him!" Instead, Little Stevie tried something else his dad had told him to do. He smiled. He smiled wide and then he began to laugh. After a second Donald started laughing too.

"What are y'all laughing at?" Barney demanded. "Stop it!"

Little Stevie laughed harder and soon all of his friends were laughing as well, even though they had no idea what they were laughing about. They knew that it was bugging Barney and his buddies and that was enough. They had all been picked on by the bullies at one time or another so they just laughed, and laughed. "Stop laughing at me!" Barney yelled. Barney got louder with his demands. "What are y'all laughing at? You better stop it!"

Little Stevie noticed that they had gotten the attention of a couple of teachers so he nudged Donald to follow him to the restroom. The rest of his table got up as well, unable to stop laughing now, and followed Little Stevie into the restroom. Barney and his bully buddies just stood there, dumbfounded by what had just happened.

"Barney, are you okay?" A teacher asked. Barney looked around to see that his back-up had all sat down and he was standing alone in the middle of the cafeteria with everybody staring at him.

"Naw." He said at first. "I mean yea," and he sat down. Everybody was still looking at him, including the teacher, so he turned his back to them and started a conversation with his buddies.

Little Stevie and his friends came out of the restroom and passed the teachers. As they walked by Stevie's math teacher, Mr Jones, called his name. All the kids at the school, including Little Stevie, thought that Mr. Jones was just a little bit scatter brained.

"Stevie!" He said. Little Stevie turned to face him. "Come here for a second please. Donald, you too please. The rest of you can go sit down." He said to the students entering his classroom.

"Little Stevie, Donald." Mr Jones looked both of them up and down. "What was all that laughing about? And why did you all go to the restroom at the same time?"

"Well." Little Stevie began. "Barney was trying to pick a fight with me, as usual, and instead of fighting him and getting my butt kicked, I tried something my Dad taught me a while back. He told me to just smile, laugh and walk away, so that's what I did."

"I suppose that *is* better than getting your butt kicked. Huh?" Mr. Jones said more to himself than to Little Stevie and Donald.

"Yes sir!" They said at the same time.

"Huh? Oh, right." Mr. Jones looked at them both with a wrinkled forehead. "Well, go take your seats boys."

Little Stevie and Donald looked at each other and then at their math teacher. "Uh, we were on our way to homeroom Mr. Jones." Said Donald.

"Oh, right!" Mr. Jones repeated and turned away.

"He seems a little confused today." Little Stevie said and giggled. "Maybe he didn't eat his Cheerios this morning."

"Yea." Snickered Donald. "What was his excuse yesterday?"

"Right. Maybe he hasn't eaten Cheerios for years." They both laughed all the way to homeroom.

***

School days seemed to go on forever, at least for Little Stevie. He was usually done with class work long before everybody else and he could only doodle so much before total boredom took over and he began to nod off. He and Donald were in Mr. Jones' math class and both of them had already finished with their assignments when Donald asked if he could go to the restroom.

"Yes, but don't dilly dally." Mr. Jones told him. "Go directly to the restroom and right back!"

"Yessir!" Replied Donald, and he got up and left. After two or three minutes Little Stevie realized that his best friend should have returned by then. Another minute passed and Mr. Jones noticed that Donald hadn't come back as well. "Little Stevie, why don't you go and see what is taking your friend so long."

"Okay Mr. Jones." Little Stevie said.

"Don't *you* get lost too!" Mr. Jones added.

"I won't!"

Little Stevie exited the classroom and turned left into the hall. Then he made a right down another hallway and he heard what sounded like a scuffle in the restroom up ahead. He sped up and when he pushed open the restroom door he saw Barney the bully and two of his bully buddies standing over Donald who was sitting on the restroom floor. Donald saw Little Stevie and tried to get up from the floor, but Barney just pushed him back down. "Let me up!" Donald said. Little Stevie saw that Donald's lip was bleeding and he knew that Barney had probably punched

Donald in the mouth. Little Stevie got mad and as Barney was turning around Little Stevie charged at him with his head down. Barney's bully buddies both grabbed Little Stevie's arms and held him before he could reach Barney.

"Let me go!" Little Stevie yelled.

"Yea! Let him go!" Donald echoed Little Stevie and tried once again to get up from the floor. As he was standing to his feet however, Barney punched him in the face again and Donald fell back to the floor.

"Umph!"

"Donald!" Little Stevie cried out to his friend. Donald sat there in shock while the two bullies held Little Stevie.

"You need to worry about yourself!" Said Barney.

"Yea! Give it to him Barney!" One of the bully buddies said.

Barney grabbed Little Stevie by his shirt collar and began shaking him and screaming. "Whatcha gonna do now little boy? Huh? Huh?" Then Barney slapped him across the jaw. Little Stevie heard a ringing in his ears and he heard one of Barney's bully buddies say that somebody was coming.

"Let's get out of here Barney!" Little Stevie heard as he hit the floor. Then he heard the sound of sneakers hitting the floor as the bullies left the restroom. Little Stevie rolled his head in Donald's direction and saw that his friend was getting up.

"Little Stevie, Donald." It was the principal, Mr. Flannagan. "What's going on here? Why are you on the floor Little Stevie?"

Then Mr. Flannagan saw Little Stevie's face. It was as red as a beet. "My goodness!" Exclaimed Mr. Flannagan. Then he looked at Donald's face as well. "What happened to your faces? Did you boys get into a fight?"

"No sir!" Stevie and Donald said at the same time.

"Well, someone needs to tell me what's going on, now!"

"I'm okay Mr. Flannagan. Really, I just want to go back to class." Said Little Stevie. He got up and shook his head to get the cobwebs out.

"Nobody's going anywhere until I find out what happened here." Mr. Flannagan replied. "So somebody had better start talking!" He just stared at the two of them. "Boys?"

Little Stevie dropped his head, but Donald couldn't help himself.

"It was Barney and those idiot friends of his!" Donald cried out. "They held me down on the floor while Barney punched me, and then they held Little Stevie while Barney slapped the fire out of *him*!"

"Donald!" Little Stevie blurted out.

"I'm sorry Stevie, but they just beat the crap out of you and me for no reason!"

"Is this true Stevie?"

"Yes sir." Little Stevie said with his head still hung low.

"Alright boys, let's go to my office." Said Mr. Flannagan. "I'm going to get to the bottom of this. Whose class are you boys supposed to be in right now?"

chapter one

"Mr. Jones' math class." replied Donald.

"Does Mr. Jones know where you are right now?"

"Well, yes sir." Little Stevie answered. "Donald came to the restroom first and when he didn't come back, Mr. Jones asked me to go look for him. That's when I, I mean *we*, got beat up by Barney and his friends."

"Well, let's stop by his classroom and let him know what's going on. Let's go boys."

Little Stevie and Donald waited in the hall while Mr. Flannagan told Mr. Jones why the boys weren't in class.

"Alright, let's get on down to my office so you can give me the *full* story." Said Mr. Flannagan. Little Stevie looked at Donald and shrugged as if to ask, "*What*?" Donald just shook his head and kept walking. When they arrived at his office Mr. Jones told Donald to wait in the chair outside of the office. "I want to talk to each of you, but one at a time. Okay?"

"Yes sir." They both answered.

When Mr. Jones was finished with Little Stevie, the boys traded places and Little Stevie sat in the chair while Donald was in the hotseat. Little Stevie noticed that the chair was warm and he wondered if Donald had farted in the chair. The thought made him a bit uncomfortable so he squirmed a little and then stood up beside the chair. After a few minutes Mr. Flannagan's door opened but only Donald came out. He didn't say anything until after the door shut.

"He called my mom dude!" Donald said in a loud whisper. "And he's gonna call your mom too!"

"What?" Asked Little Stevie. "Are you kidding me?"

"Naw man. He told my mom right there in front of me that you and me were involved in some kind of ongoing problem with some other kids and that he wasn't sure who started what or who was bullying who and blah, blah, blah."

Little Stevie just shook his head. "What the crap?"

""Yea, I know. Right?" Said Donald. "It's like he doesn't believe us or something."

"Well, is he going to call Barney and those other morons to the office and see if they have any bruises or red marks on their faces?" Little Stevie wanted to know.

"I don't know." Said Donald. "He didn't say. He just said that he had to call my parents and your parents because we were the only ones in the restroom looking suspicious. Can you believe that?"

"Humph!" Little Stevie snorted. "Can we at least go back to class now?"

"No. Mr. Flannagan said for us to just wait out here until he got to the bottom of things." Donald made quotation marks with his fingers on both sides of his head. "Whatever that means."

Mr. Flannagan's office door opened halfway and he leaned out. "Little Stevie, I've just spoken to your mother as well as

Donald's, they will both be here at the end of fifth period today. You boys can go on back to class."

"What about Barney and the rest of them?" Little Stevie asked. "We're the ones that got be…"

"You let me worry about *that* young man." Mr. Flannagan replied before Little Stevie could finish. "Get on to class now."

"Yes sir." Answered Little Stevie.

"Yes sir." Said Donald.

Math class was over by the time Little Stevie and Donald walked into Mr. Jones' classroom. They just had time to get their books and homework assignments before lunch began. "What are you going to have for lunch Stevie?" Donald asked as they rounded the corner and entered the cafeteria.

"I don't know, what are they having?"

"Uh, yea." Said Donald. "Today's Monday. They're having pizza and taco salad in line one."

"Oh yea?"

"Yea. And it's baked chicken and spaghetti in line two." Said Donald. "You know there's a bulletin board beside the office door."

"Yea." Little Stevie replied. "So."

"Well, every Monday they post the entire week's menu on it. Soon after that somebody usually tears it down, but it's there for a minute anyway."

"Oh yea? I have noticed a big empty square spot on the bulletin board from time to time." Said Little Stevie. "I guess I'll have to look at it on Monday, before somebody like Barney tears it down."

"Yea, that's what I do." Said Donald. "Because we all know that lunch is one of my favorite subjects!"

"Yea, I get it. You love to eat."

"Hey I've seen you put away ten hot wings at one time, so don't get all uppity just because you're so short!"

"Whoa there neighbor!" Exclaimed Little Stevie with a grin. "There's no reason to bring height into it! It's not my fault that I'm vertically challenged!"

"Okay, okay." Said Donald. "I'm sorry. That was a *low blow*!"

"Ouch!" Little Stevie said. "Nice one! You're full of 'em today. Aren't you?"

"Yea, I was kinda proud of that one." Donald said with a wide smile.

"Oh, did I say full of *them*?" Little Stevie came back. "I meant full of *it*!"

They laughed while they made their lunch choices known to the lunch ladies. They both decided on baked chicken, got their trays and sat down at their usual table with their usual friends. They noticed right away that the bully table where Barney and his buddies sat was completely empty, and the rumors started flying. The most interesting one was that Little Stevie and Donald had beaten them all up at once in the restroom and that they all were taken to the hospital for treatment.

A couple of kids came over to their table and gave Stevie and Donald pats on the back and told them, "good for you," or "way to go." One of their group finally told Little Stevie and Donald about the rumors.

"What?" Little asked.

"Yea!" Echoed Donald as he pointed at Little Stevie "What he said!"

"Yea man." Said their friend Jimmy. "It's all over the school. The story is that you and Donald here whipped the tar out of Barney and two or three of his friends in the restroom over by the gym."

"Well that's not what happened!" Said Donald. "It's the other way around! We're the ones that got beat up, but nobody had to go to the hospital for crying out loud!"

"Yea." Little Stevie said. "This is what happened." He told the whole story to his friends and when he was done they all looked over at the bully table.

"Well, where are they?" Jimmy asked.

"They are probably all in Mr. Flannagan's office. He said he was gonna take care of it after he, *got to the bottom of things!*" Donald did his best impression of the principal and it cracked up everyone at the table.

"Donald!" It was Mr. Flannagan. "Aw crap!" Donald thought to himself.

"You and Little Stevie come to my office when you finish lunch. We're going to settle this thing between you two and Barney, today!"

Little Stevie and Donald looked at one another. "Yes sir." They answered.

Mr. Flannagan turned and exited the cafeteria. "What about the rest of those idiots?" Donald asked out loud. "I wonder if he brought *all* of them up to his office."

"Well, there not in the cafeteria, that's for sure." Jimmy said.

"Yea, that's true." Said Little Stevie. "But he only mentioned Barney."

"Yea." Donald said and looked down at his tray. "I'm done Little Stevie. I'm not even hungry anymore. You ready to go and get this over with?"

"We might as well. Let's go and put our trays up."

The two of them made their way to the office and arrived to find only Barney in Mr. Flannagan's office.

"Come in and close the door boys." Mr Flannagan said as they appeared in his doorway. Barney was sitting in the chair on the far left in front of the principal's desk and there were two other chairs as well.

"Have a seat." Mr. Flannagan told them. "Here's the situation guys. Barney has already confessed to his part in what happened. He told me about the problems that he and you guys have had in the past and how what happened in the restroom was partly his fault."

Little Stevie and Donald looked at each other in disbelief.

"*Partly* his fault?! Little Stevie asked while leaning forward in his seat. "*They*, not just him, but *they*, started the whole thing. Him and that whole gang of his beat the crap out of us for no reason at all!"

"Don't raise your voice in my office young man!" Mr. Flannagan told Little Stevie. "Barney is here to make things right between you three and I think you should just shake hands and be done with all of this nonsense!"

"Are you kidding me?" Asked Donald. "What about the rest of them? It wasn't just Barney you know! They all jumped on me in the restroom and when Little Stevie came in to check on me, two of them held him and Barney slapped in across the face. He knocked him down, and if Mr. Jones hadn't come looking for the both of us, there's no telling what they might have done to us!"

"Who is *they*, Donald? And I'm not going to tell either of you again to not raise your voice to me!"

"I'm sorry Mr. Flannagan. It was Barney and his buddies. Jeffrey, Billy and I don't know that other guy's name, but they jumped me first in the restroom and then Little Stevie when he came to check on me."

"Well Barney came to my office on his own and told me a completely different story." Mr. Flannagan asserted. "Why should I believe your side of it instead of his?"

"Look at my face!" Exclaimed Little Stevie. "Look at Donald's nose! We didn't come to school looking like this! He and his friends did this to us for no reason at all!" Little Stevie pointed his finger at Barney. "He's lying Mr. Flannagan! Look at how big he is, and look at me. They call me Little Stevie for a reason!"

"Don't get that tone with me boy!" The principal growled. "You're in enough trouble as it is!"

"For what?" Little Stevie asked in much calmer voice. "I'll just wait until my mom gets here before I say anything else."

"Your parents aren't coming. I called them back and told them that there was no need for them to come all the way to the school because we had this all worked out. Obviously I was wrong."

"Yes sir." replied Little Stevie. "I would like to call my mom now please."

"So would I." Said Donald.

Mr. Flannagan stared at them both for a second, but he knew that by law he could not deny them the opportunity to call home if they were sick or if there was a disciplinary issue.

"Okay boys." He said and pushed the telephone on his desk across to them.

"Barney, you can go back to class now." Barney didn't say a word, he simply got up and left the office.

"I hope you realize what kind of problems you are creating." Mr. Flannagan said.

"We didn't do anything wrong." Little Stevie told him as he dialed his home number.

Fifteen minutes later both Little Stevie's mother and Donald's mother were in the principal's office. Little Stevie and Donald waited outside in the same chairs as before and they could hear both of their moms giving Mr. Flannagan "down the country" for not calling them when he saw the marks on their son's faces.

"I'm taking my son home for the remainder of the day, if that's alright with you sir!" Little Stevie heard his mom say, followed by Donald's mom. "My son will be leaving early today as well!"

"Ladies, please. If you would just..." Mr. Flannagan tried to speak but was cut off by two angry moms.

"If something like this ever happens again, you *will* have to tell a judge why you didn't feel it necessary to inform the parents of their children's injuries!" Little Stevie's mom shrieked as she stormed out of the office followed by Donald's mom. Little Stevie's mom was friends with one of the county judges and both ladies were well respected in the local PTA.

"Let's go home boys." Donald's mom said.

"Early release day today?" Donald joked.

"Yea." Little Stevie said. "Maybe we oughta get beat up more often." Both boys laughed, with scornful looks from both moms.

When Little Stevie got home he went to check on the rooster. His dad and he had put the rooster in his fox proof coop that morning before Little Stevie had left for school. The rooster got excited when he saw Little Stevie and began strutting around the coop and flapping it's wings. It crowed a couple of times and rushed out with it's wings flapping, running circles around Little Stevie after he opened the gate and let him out. The rooster continued to follow Little Stevie around like a puppy dog just like before, except the rooster was strong and healthy this time and he even appeared to have grown some in the last few weeks. It stood at least two and one half feet tall and had a thick strong looking chest with sharp two inch long spurs on it's feet. Little Stevie still liked to feed the rooster from his hand, but it hurt just a little since it had regained it's strength so he put gloves on whenever he could. He and his rooster walked around the property for a half an hour or so before mom called Little Stevie in for supper. Big Steve had just arrived home too and Little Stevie couldn't wait to tell his dad about what happened at school.

So, tell me about what happened to you and Donald at school today." Big Steve told his son. "Your mom said that there was a problem with that kid named Barney, and the principal."

"Yes sir." Replied Little Stevie. "I think Barney knew that he was gonna get into trouble, so he went to the principal and told him a bunch of lies after we already told him what happened."

"Well, tell *me* what happened."

"Okay. Well, Donald went to the restroom, and when he didn't come back right away, Mr. Jones told me to go look for him and see what was taking him so long. When I got to the restroom, I saw Donald on the floor, and his lip was bleeding. I tried to help him and two guys grabbed me and held my arms. Then this big bully, Barney, slapped me so hard across my jaw that it made my ears ring. That's when Mr. Flannagan came in and found me on the floor with Donald trying to help me up."

"What happened to the boys that attacked you?"

"Oh, they heard Mr. Flannagan coming, I think, and took off."

"Let me see your face son." Big Steve said and gently put his hand on Little Stevie's jaw. Little Stevie turned his head and Big *Steve's* face turned red with anger.

"Did the principal see your face? Was it bruised up like this in his office?"

"No sir, but it was as red as a beet. And Donald's lip was busted and bleeding!"

"And Mr. Flannagan thinks that this is something you and Donald might have started?!" Big Steve asked with a tone that scared mom and Little Stevie. Big Steve saw the reaction on his son's face and calmed his voice. "It's okay son, just tell me what Mr. Flannagan said."

"Well, he said that Barney came to his office on his own and told him what happened after we already told him, the real story I mean."

"Go on son."

"He said that Barney was willing to shake hands and forget about the trouble that *we* had been causing and make things right, or something like that."

"And this is the same Barney that you've been having all these problems with all year long?" Asked Big Steve.

"Yes sir."

"And have you told anybody about this at school?"

"Yes sir, a couple of times." Said Little Stevie.

"I'm going to take you to school tomorrow." Said Big Steve. "I know you think it will make things worse, and you don't want me to but…"

"Oh no dad." Replied Little Stevie. "I want you to go talk to Mr. Flannagan. I want you to ask him why he didn't believe Donald or me, but he believed that big bully who gets into trouble all the time."

"Oh." Said Big Steve. "Alright then. Now you're sure that you didn't do anything to provoke this Barney kid? You nor Donald?"

"Dad!"

"Yea, right. Dumb question." Said Big Steve. "Does your jaw hurt?"

"No, not really. How does it look?"

"You look like you've been in a title fight, and lost!" They both laughed. "Hey, how is Donald? Does he look as bad as you?"

"Well, he's got a fat lip, and I've got a bruised jaw." Said Little Stevie. "I guess we look about the same."

"What about his parents?" Big Steve asked his wife. "Are they going to the school tomorrow too?"

"Oh yes!" Mom said. "Donald's mom was there at the same time as me today and we let him have it, but I think you and Craig will make a better impression on him than two helpless little ladies." Mom laughed and Little Stevie said, "You didn't sound helpless from out in the hallway."

"Oh, did you gals give Mr. Flannagan a hard time today?" Big Steve asked with a sly grin on his face.

"He knew that we were serious. That's all I'm going to say."

***

That next morning Big Steve took Little Stevie to school just like he said he would.

"I need to see Mr. Flannagan please." He told the receptionist at the desk in the front of the office. "Yes sir." She replied and picked up her phone. "There is a gentleman requesting to see you sir." She said to Mr. Flannagan on the other end. "Yes sir." She said and hung up the telephone. "Right this way sir." Big Steve and Little Stevie got up and followed her down a narrow hallway. Halfway down she stopped and turned around. "Little

Stevie, you can go on to homeroom now." Little Stevie looked at his dad.

"No ma'am, he's going with me." Big Steve told her.

"But homeroom will be star…" She began.

"I said, he's with me!" Big Steve reasserted.

"Oh, yes sir. I'm sorry sir." And sugar wouldn't have melted in her mouth at that moment. "Mr. Flannagan, the gentleman to see you sir." She said after knocking on the office door.

"Thank you Denise." Mr. Flannagan said and she walked back to her desk. Mr. Flannagan saw Little Stevie and told him he could wait out in the hall.

"No sir!" Big Steve said with a hint of irritation in his voice. "This is my son, and he is the reason I wanted to speak to you sir."

"Yes, of course but usually I speak wi…"

"I don't care what you usually do *Mr.* Flannagan!" Big Steve cut *him* off too. "My son tells me that he and his friend Donald were jumped and beat up by three or four of your school bullies, and you are trying to put some of the blame for that on them!"

"Well that is a matter that I'm still looking into and…" He began as Big Steve and Little Stevie sat down.

"Did the other boys have any marks on them?" Big Steve wanted to know. "Did they?" Big Steve got louder. "Stand up son." He said to Little Stevie. He turned Little Stevie around so the principal could see the side of his face where Barney had slapped him. "Do you see that? That's what this Barney the bully did to my son! What have you done about it?"

There was a knock on the office door. "Yes Denise." The door opened and there was Donald and his dad. Like Big Steve, Donald's dad was rather large and scary to those who didn't know him. His name was Craig and he was just as upset as Big Steve about what happened at school the day before.

"I want to know what you are doing about my son's busted lip Mr. Flannagan!" Craig asked forcefully.

"Oh, he's still looking into it Craig!" Big Steve said. "Why don't you come on in and we can *get to the bottom of it* together!" Craig and Donald stepped into the office and Craig closed the door. "Now!" Craig said looking directly at Mr. Flannagan. "What are you going to do about these two boys getting jumped yesterday?"

"Well I…" Mr. Flannagan started.

"And don't tell me that you're looking into it! You already know what happened, because I know that Steve has already given you the facts!"

"Oh yes!" Said Big Steve. "Yes I have! And based on those facts, I want you to tell us right now, what you intend to do about that gang of thugs that seem to get away with doing whatever they want in this school!"

"Or maybe I'll just go to the next school board meeting, and PTA meeting and tell everybody I know that you are not able to keep these kids safe and that maybe we need someone else to oversee the education of our children!" Added Craig.

He and Big Steve then both stood over Mr. Flannagan's desk and Big Steve leaned in real close so neither Little Stevie nor Donald could hear him. "If anything else happens to either of these boys again at school, if they so much as fall off of the jungle gym or slip in some spilled milk in the cafeteria, I will hold *you*, personally responsible. Do you understand me?"

Mr. Flannagan sighed heavily and nodded. Then he picked his desk phone and spoke to his secretary Denise. He instructed her to call up Barney and the other three bullies that attacked Little Stevie and Donald. "They will be suspended for a week, starting today." He told Big Steve and Craig. "And when they come back they will be placed in in-school suspension for the remainder of the school year. They will be watched very closely and they won't be allowed to go near your boys, while they're at school." He added. "How's that?"

"Good enough." Replied Big Steve. "For the time being."

"Yea." Craig growled. "That will do for now."

Big Steve and Craig, along with Little Stevie and Donald left the principal's office just as Barney and the others were coming down the hall. Craig held the door open for Barney and his crew but stared at them real hard as they entered. "Hey Little Stevie!" Barney said nervously when he saw how big the two men were. Barney knew that he was in big trouble and all of a sudden he wanted to make friends with Little Stevie and Donald. The two boys didn't even look at him, they just held their heads high and ignored Barney and his bully buddies.

Later that day more rumors were going around that Big Steve and Craig had roughed up Mr. Flannagan until he was so scared that he decided to suspend Barney and the other bullies. There were also rumors that Barney was sent to a youth detention center for six months, and that Barney and his "crew" were "whacked" by some hitmen. At the lunch table however Little Stevie and Donald told everybody what really happened and the horror stories ended. "So when are those morons coming back to school?" Jimmy asked before cramming half a hotdog into his mouth.

"Well, they're suspended for a week, but they will have to go to ISS for the rest of the year when they come back." Said Little Stevie.

"No kiddin?" Said their friend Trey. "You mean we get to spend the remainder of the school year, bully free?"

"That's right!" Said Donald. "Almost six whole months, idiot free!"

"Yes yes." Little Stevie added. "Six months, no morons."

"Uh uh." Jimmy said. "Y'all are forgetting about Mr. Jones."

"He's right." Trey spoke up. "Mr. Jones is usually *way* out there somewhere."

"Yes." Said Little Stevie. "But has Mr. Jones ever punched any of us in the face?"

"Little Stevie has a good point there guys." Replied Trey.

"Hey!" Donald suddenly said and jumped up from his seat. "Why don't we have a party in honor of the temporary loss of the idiot, bully, morons, from now on known as the...idullyrons! Yes, the idullyrons!" He repeated.

"That's a great idea Donald!" Said Little Stevie. "That's a great new word too. We gotta write that one down. Somebody give me a piece of paper!" Donald tore out a sheet of paper from his notebook and Little Stevie pulled an ink pen from his shirt pocket. "Now, we can have the party at my house, in my garage." He added after writing down the newly created word. "And we'll call it the idullyron party!"

"Let me see how y'all spell that!" Said Trey. "I'm gonna write that down too, and then I'll make up some invitation cards and hand them out to all our friends. Hey, when *is* the party?"

"Well, let me talk to my mom and dad this afternoon and we'll decide after that." Little Stevie said. "How about we shoot for Saturday afternoon. Everybody okay with that?"

They all agreed that Saturday was a good day for the celebration and that Little Stevie's house was the place for the party. Trey began making the invitation cards with the title, "idullyron party" and later on, in the car rider line, Jimmy came up with the idea of having a contest to see if anyone could guess how they came up with the word idullyron. Donald rode home with

Little Stevie and on the ride home Little Stevie asked his mom about the party.

"Mom." He began.

"Yes honey."

"You remember the bullies that roughed Donald and me up?"

"Don't you mean Donald and I?" Mom corrected him.

"What?" Little Stevie asked. "Did you get beat up too?"

Mom shook her head and stopped at a stop sign. She turned and looked at Little Stevie and Donald. "What?" She asked with a puzzled look on her face. Little Stevie and Donald covered turned their heads to keep mom from seeing the mile wide grins they had. Then she got it.

"Smarty pants!" She snapped with a smile. "Y'all know what I mean."

"Yes ma'am!" Replied Donald. "I was just going along with my best friend here. I really had nothing to do with it. He's the real smarty pants!"

"Ouch! Pull it out! Pull it out!" Little Stevie cried.

"What's wrong with *you*?" Mom asked. "And pull what out?"

"The knife that my best pal just stuck in my back!"

"Oh, Stevie. You *are* a smarty pants!" Mom said as she crossed the intersection. "Now what were you asking me before you got the knife in your back?"

"What? Oh yea. We, and I mean *we,* were wanting to know if *we*, could have a little get together at the house in the garage on Saturday. It's a celebration, sort of."

"A celebration?" She wrinkled her forehead. "A celebration for what? And what was that you said about that gang of hooligans that beat you and Donald up?"

"That's what we want to celebrate. We're going to be completely idiot, bully, moron free for the rest of the school year and we just wanted to have a little party in honor of that freedom."

"The rest of the year? I thought that they were only suspended for a week."

"Didn't dad tell you?" Asked Little Stevie. They all got ISS for the rest of the year, when they come back. Isn't it wonderful?" Little Stevie sighed like a girl and fanned himself with his hand.

"You've been watching Gone With The Wind again, haven't you?" Asked Donald

"Uh, yea!" Little Stevie answered with the deepest manly voice he could muster. "WHAT ABOUT IT?" He asked with all the bass he could.

They all laughed as mom turned the car into the driveway. "Yes, I suppose a party would be alright, as long as your dad says it's okay." She said.

"Thanks mom!" Little Stevie said.

Little Stevie and Donald went around to the chicken coop and let the rooster out. It acted very excited to see Little Stevie and even flew up to perch on his arm like he had done before.

"What are you going to do when he craps on your arm?" Donald wanted to know.

"I don't know." Replied Little Stevie. "I haven't thought about that. He hasn't done it yet though."

"Well, I want you to know that I'm here for you." Said Donald. "But I won't be cleaning your arm up for you when it happens. Oh, and I'll probably laugh, a lot. And if I happen to have a camera nearby, I'm gonna take a picture of it, and show it to all our friends. *And,* I'll be reminding you of it everytime I see you."

"What a pal, what a pal!" Little Stevie said and slapped Donald on the back twice.

"Stevie!" Mom called from the front door of the house. "You've got some chores to do!"

"I know mom! I'll be there in just a couple of minutes!" He yelled back. He put the rooster back into the chicken coop and made sure the door was secure.

"That reminds me." Said Donald. "I've got a few things to take care of myself, so I'm gonna head on home too."

"Okay man, try to come up with some ideas for the party, you know some games or something for when we run out of food and things to talk about."

"What?" Exclaimed Donald. "Me and you and the guys never run out of cool stuff to talk about!" Remember that time that we…"

"Hopefully," Little Stevie cut him off. "There will be chicks there, and they like to talk about different things than we do. *And,* they like to play games and other stuff, *and*, I don't want to have a lame party that people will be talking about for weeks. Ya know what I mean?"

"I got ya bro. I'll work on that. Talk to ya later."

"See ya Big D."

"Big D?" Donald asked. "My dad used to call me that."

"Yea, I know. I just remembered it."

"Yea, okay." Said Donald. "See ya Little S."

Little Stevie wrinkled his forehead, then shook his head. "Nah, that doesn't really work."

"Nah." Agreed Donald. "It doesn't, does it?" He turned and started walking. "Gotta go man. I'll see you in the morning!"

"See ya Big D!"

After supper that night Little Stevie's mom called him into the living room. He was finishing his homework when he heard his mom call his name. "Stevie! Would you come down here for a minute? Your dad and I would like to talk to you!"

"Yes ma'am! I'm coming. Just let me put my homework up!"

"Oh, I'm sorry honey. You can finish it first!" Mom called out.

"No, I'm done mom." He answered. "I just have to put it up now! Give me just a second please!"

"Okay!"

A couple of seconds later Little Stevie came running down the stairs. "What can I do for you two fine examples of parenthood?" He plopped down on the sofa between his mom and dad. "You really *are* fine parents you know?"

"Yea, yea, yea." Big Steve said dryly. "You can have your party so quit sucking up!"

"Alright Big Steve! Mr. Super Cool!"

"Alright!" Said Big Steve. "Calling them like you see them. Now that's more like it!"

"Mr. Super Cool? And what am I?" Mom asked. "Miss Chopped liver?"

"Oh no mom. You're more like...Miss, or should I say, Mrs. America!"

"Okay Stevie, that's just a little, uh, okay, dead on if you say so!"

"I'll second that!" Said Big Steve. "Mrs. America!"

Little Stevie and Big Steve began clapping and whistling with chants like "Hip, hip, hooray!" and "Three cheers for Mrs. America!"

"Okay, okay. It's getting a little deep in here!" Mom said. "I'll give you ten or fifteen minutes to stop all that craziness!"

"Okay mom, we'll stop now." Said Little Stevie. "We were just kiddin around anyway."

Oh no, no no!" Mom said with half a smile. "You've still got ten or fifteen minutes."

"Now let's talk about this party!" Big Steve said. "How many people are we talking about?"

"I don't know." Replied Little Stevie. "Ten or twelve I guess. Maybe a couple more."

"Okay, have you got your activities all planned out?"

"Donald and I are working on that."

"Do you have a list of kids you are going to invite?"

"I'm working on that too." Replied Little Stevie. "And, I know what kind of food and refreshments I want to have also, so we've got everything almost worked out."

"Well alrighty then." Said Big Steve. "You just let me and Mrs. America know if there's anything we can do."

"I will. Thanks Dad."

"Oh, I almost forgot." Big Steve said. "*When* are you going to throw this party?"

"Saturday afternoon,"

"Okay. Good enough then. Make sure you let us know by tomorrow how many people are going to be here, so we can be sure to have enough food for everybody."

"Yessir!"

The rest of the week passed by quickly enough and before Little Stevie knew it, the party was on. A total of sixteen kids, including Little Stevie, were there to enjoy the festivities in the garage. Big Steve let the kids use his own personal portable stereo that included a CD player as well as an AM/FM radio. Mom had supplied the food and when she did something, she did it up right. There was pizza, hot wings, tortilla chips with three kinds of dip, chilli cheese fries, ice cream, cheesecake and five different flavors of soda.

The kids played games too. It started out with simple games like charades and some trivial pursuit, but then when the grownups said that they were going watch some TV in the bedroom and leave the kids alone for a while, the young ladies on the scene decided that they were going to play either truth or dare, or spin the bottle. Of course the guys had heard of the games before and a couple of them had even played once or twice, but when the girls all seemed to agree at once on playing truth or dare first, and then spin the bottle, the boys got all nervous and jittery. They all began to look around at one another as if they were unsure of what to do or what to say.

"Unless you boys are chicken, or something!" A girl named Tammy said. Teasing the boys.

"Yea. What's the matter?" Said Anita, another one of the girls at the party. "You afraid you might have to *kiss* one of us or something?"

Actually, most of the boys were terrified of that very thing happening. Not one of them *had* ever kissed a girl before, and the first kiss was a *big* deal. Nobody wanted to be known as the guy with the lame lips but Little Stevie was not going to be known as a chicken either.

"I'm not chicken!" He said boldly. "Just let me get my lips ready!" Little Stevie began moving his lips around like he was exercising them. Then he made motorboat sounds and fart noises until they all were laughing. The comedy act put everyone at ease and in only a couple of minutes the telltale game was on. Jimmy found a soda bottle and eight or nine of the group sat down in a circle in the middle of the garage while the others danced or hung around the refreshments. Jimmy laid the bottle on the cement floor and gave it a test spin.

"Are we playing truth or dare, or spin the bottle?" Donald asked when the bottle stopped spinning.

"Well, it's basically the same thing isn't it?" Tammy asked. Nobody was one hundred percent sure so everybody just nodded their heads and agreed.

"Here's what we'll do!" Said Little Stevie. "Whoever spins the bottle gets to ask truth or dare to whoever it lands on. Okay?"

Everyone thought that was fair and the game began. Little Stevie was the first to spin and it landed on a girl named Jenny. Jenny gasped with surprise, as girls will do, and told Little Stevie to go ahead with his question.

"Okay." Said Little Stevie. "Truth or dare?" Jenny looked around at the other girls in the circle and back at Little Stevie.

"Uh, truth." She finally said.

"Okay, is it true that you've kissed a boy on the lips before?"

"Oh my God!" Jenny said. "Little Stevie!"

"You have to answer the question truthfully Jenny!" Donald barked out.

"I know. I know!" Jenny hesitated. "Y'all quit staring at me!"

"Come on Jenny." Jimmy teased. "It's not that big of a deal."

"Yea come on." Donald added. "It's a simple question."

"Okay, no!" Jenny said. "I've never kissed a boy on the lips before! Are you happy?" She glanced at Little Stevie at the same time that he was looking at her. Little Stevie quickly looked away when their eyes met but they both noticed the other and there was a connection. It was one of those things that you just know and Little Stevie was very happy when Jenny had announced the uncomfortable truth about never having kissed a boy on the lips before. Little Stevie had noticed Jenny before but since they were both just a little shy, the two of them had never shared a private conversation. This was perfect for Little Stevie.

"Next!" Jenny belted out. "Stop staring at *me* now!"

"Well, who goes next? I mean who spins the bottle?" Asked Trey.

"I think it goes around to the right." Said Little Stevie. "So Tammy spins next."

"Alrighty then!" Said Donald. "Let's get that bottle spinnin and find out the ugly truth about somebody else!"

Tammy spun the bottle and it landed on Little Stevie. "Ahh."
Tammy said while nodding her head. "Truth or dare Little Stevie?"
Little Stevie wasn't up for a dare yet, especially from a girl.

"Truth." He answered.

"Okay." Tammy said. "I'll keep it simple. Have *you* ever kissed
a girl on the lips before?"

"No." Answered Little Stevie. Then he added, "But it wasn't
because I didn't want to!" And he automatically looked over at
Jenny. He looked away quickly enough but a couple of the others,
including Jenny and Tammy, noticed it.

"Donald's turn! And give it a good spin Big D!" Said Trey.

"Here we go!" Said Donald. The bottle spun for twenty or so
seconds before it came to rest with the open end pointing at a
girl named Kayla.

"Kayla! Truth or dare?" Donald asked while rubbing his hands
together like an old movie villain.

Everybody was staring at Kayla but Little Stevie was thinking
about Jenny. He couldn't help himself. He had given her some
passing thoughts before but never like the ones he was having
right then. He was warm and fuzzy all over and his heart must
have been beating a hundred beats a minute. He wanted to
kiss her. He wanted her to be his first kiss. He knew it and he
found himself hoping that she knew it too. What he didn't know
was that Tammy knew, and she had devised a plan to help Little

Stevie out with his problem. But first, she had to wait for her turn to spin the bottle again.

"Dare!" Kayla blurted out finally.

"Oooh!" Donald squealed. "A dare. Finally! I dare you to...uh, uh, to stand up and do a thirty second hokey pokey with Trey's glasses on!"

"Really?" She asked with disbelief.

"Oh yes. Really!"

So she did a thirty second hokey pokey dance wearing Trey's eye glasses. When she turned herself around is when it got entertaining. Kayla staggered and stumbled like a drunk monkey and would have fallen if Donald hadn't stood up with her and helped her keep her balance.

"My hero!" Kayla said and gave Donald a hug. Then she took off the glasses and gave them back to Trey. Everyone got a big kick out of Kayla's hokey pokey dance but she was more than ready to sit down and give the stage to somebody else.

"Next victim!" Donald said.

"Trey's turn to spin the bottle!" Jenny pointed out. Two of the kids that had chosen to dance instead of play changed their minds and joined the game and the rest of that group gathered around the circle and watched. The truths that were being told seemed to be getting juicier and the dares were a little more interesting so no one wanted to miss a thing.

Trey spun the bottle and it landed on Donald. "Truth or Dare Big D?" Trey asked.

"Truth!" Donald replied. "It *will* set you free!"

"Okay man." Trey began. "That hug that Kayla gave you a while ago. Was that just a friendly hug, or did you get all warm and fuzzy?"

"Yea man!" Echoed Joey from the outside circle. "Are you in *love* now?"

Donald just turned to look at Kayla. Then he cocked one eyebrow. "The jig is up, and the news is out." Donald then looked back at the rest of them. "We're getting married next week and you're all invited to the wedding!"

"That doesn't answer the question man!" Trey pointed at Donald. "Out with it!"

"Yea Big D, play the game right!" Jenny said, hoping to catch Little Stevie looking at her again.

"Anytime now!" Little Stevie chimed in.

"Okay! Okay!" Donald gave in. "Yea, I got all warm and a little sweaty from the hug. You could say that it was very pleasant. And if it happened again, I probably wouldn't run away screaming."

"I would say that was a thumbs up for you Kayla. He enjoyed it." Joey said to Kayla and put his hand up to her face as if he were holding a microphone. "Any comments for the crowd ma'am?"

"Oh yes!" Kayla said with a southern belle way of talking. "Bite me! And thank y'all very much!"

Everyone was rolling with laughter at Kayla's joke. The bottle had come back around to Tammy again and when she spun the bottle it landed on Little Stevie.

"Truth or dare?" Tammy asked him looking directly into his eyes. She made a slight gesture with her eyes in Jenny's direction and Little Stevie followed her lead.

"Dare!" He said

"Wow!" Tammy said." Are we getting brave Little Stevie? Let's see, what would be a good dare for you?" She scratched a fake itch on her head. "I know. You kiss Jenny, on the lips, if she doesn't mind."

All eyes turned to Jenny and she was feeling the heat. She didn't know what to say, so said what she was thinking. "Hey, rules are rules! So, you do what you gotta do!" She was trying to save face by being funny, so she looked at Little Stevie. "Just make it quick, please."

"You won't feel a thing." Said Little Stevie. The truth was however that they were both feeling things that they had never experienced before, but neither could reveal it to the others. Little Stevie positioned himself on the floor on his knees in front of Jenny and when he gazed into her big brown eyes he got very nervous and very hot at the same time. His hands began sweating and he was scared to death. He was excited as well however and wouldn't take back the dare for anything in the world. This was his first kiss. They leaned in close to one another and closed their eyes. It seemed to take forever and Little Stevie had to open his eyes slightly to make sure he was going in the right direction. Almost there! He reached out his hands and his fingers touched Jenny's, halfway there. They grabbed each other's hands and continued moving their lips toward one another's. When they finally made contact Little Stevie thought that Jenny's lips were the sweetest and softest things he had ever tasted before. It only lasted two or three seconds but for Little Stevie it was a lifetime. Little Stevie's heart felt like it was going to explode right out of his chest and when they separated it took Little Stevie another second or two to open his eyes again. There was an awkward silence in the garage and Donald finally spoke up.

"Wow!" He said. "Was that the kiss of the century or what?" He started clapping and cheering until the rest of the group joined in. They were so loud at that point that mom and dad came into the garage to see what all the ruckus was about. Little Stevie was a little worried about his parents finding out what they were doing but then he saw the trivial pursuit game still on the floor and he breathed a little easier.

"That must have been some question that somebody just answered!" Big Steve said when he entered the garage. "We heard the celebration from in the living room! Just checking on you guys." Big Steve stood there another second longer but nobody said a word. "Bye!" He said and darted back into the house.

"Okay, playtime's over with." Little Stevie said. "That, was just way too close."

"Yea." Agreed Trey. "Big Steve is just too big, and scary! What do you think he would do if he had caught one of us?"

"Caught us doing what?" Asked Donald. "It was just a little truth or dare!"

"Nah, I'm with Trey on this one Donald." Said Little Stevie. "I think we should quit while we're ahead!"

"Ah, ya bunch of girls!" Mocked Donald. "Hey I know what we can do! Little Stevie, show everybody your rooster!"

"Hmm. Okay." Little Stevie said. "Come on guys, he's out here." Everyone followed Little Stevie around to the back of the garage. The rooster flapped his wings when he saw all of the kids and then crowed. When Little Stevie stepped to the front of the group however the rooster flapped even harder, cackled some and crowed again.

"What do you do with a rooster?" Trey asked what they were all thinking.

"I'm still trying to figure that one out!" Replied Little Stevie. "But it's fun while you're doing the figuring. Just watch!" Little Stevie opened the gate to the chicken coop and the rooster seemed extra happy to be getting out for a while. He ran straight out the gate when it was opened and slid on a pile of leaves when he tried to stop too suddenly. All of the gang got a laugh out of it but when the rooster got his balance again he steadied himself and did a one hundred and eighty degree turn. He then raced back in the direction from whence he came and most of the kids actually thought that the rooster was coming after them for laughing at him. Girls, and boys were scrambling for any place to go to get out of the way of what they thought was rooster with an attitude brought on by being the butt of somebody's joke.

"Really you guys?" Little Stevie asked with disbelief in his voice, when Tammy told him why they all ran for their lives. "I'm pretty sure he doesn't care if y'all laugh at him or not. It's a *rooster*!"

"Yea, but he was running and flapping and clucking, and coming right at us!" Jimmy said, still catching his breath.

"Yea, but he's just a rooster, who wouldn't hurt anybody, for crying out loud."

"Hang on there Stevie!" Donald said and then whispered something in Little Stevie's ear.

"Okay!" Belted out Little Stevie. "He wouldn't hurt anybody as long as nobody tries to hurt me, or acts like they're going to hurt me!" Donald had reminded Little Stevie of how crazy the rooster acted when Donald or Big Steve pretended to hit Little Stevie.

"What? You got you a bodyguard or something?" Trey asked after Donald told them how the rooster protected Little Stevie.

"Nah man." Answered Little Stevie. "It's just a rooster."

"Yea man!" Said Donald. "Only it's like a guard dog! It's a, a, guard rooster! Yea, a guard rooster!" He repeated and everybody liked the name guard rooster. The kids got louder and they all broke off into their individual conversation groups to give their own personal opinion on the "guard rooster." The rooster sensed the excitement in the air and began to go from group to group cackling, clucking and flapping his wings as if in agreement with everything that was said.

"Oh my gosh! Guys!" Donald suddenly exclaimed. "Little Stevie, do that arm thing. You know, that thing where he flies up and lands on your arm!"

"I'll try. But I don't know if he'll do it with all these people around."

"Aw, come on!" Said Tammy. "Do it!"

"Yea!" Everyone agreed. "Do it! Do it! Do it! Do it!" They all began chanting.

"Okay! Okay!" Little Stevie looked around for the rooster.

"He's right behind you!"

"Oh. So he is!" Little replied. He held out his arm in front of him. "Come on big guy!" Little said to his rooster. The rooster crowed and flapped his wings, kneeled and flew straight up. He landed on Little Stevie's arm and sat there perched like a king on his throne. Several "oohs" and "ahs" were heard from the crowd of fascinated children as Little Stevie stood there with a rooster on his arm that was almost as big as he was.

The kids all agreed that it was a great party and thanked Little Stevie's mom for inviting them and for cooking all that delicious food. A few of Little Stevie's closest friends, along with their parents, stuck around to help out with all of the after party cleaning.

"Man, that rooster is something else!" Trey said as he, Donald and Little Stevie each carried a bag of trash out of the garage. "Did he really try to spur your dad."

"Yea he did!" Donald interrupted.

"Well, the rooster was actually in a pen in the garage at the time." Little Stevie glanced at Donald. "But my dad said that spurring is how a rooster defends itself, and that it might have spurred him if it could have gotten out."

"For hitting you?" Asked Trey.

"No. My dad and I were boxing, and the rooster didn't even like it if my dad pretended to act like he was just thinking about trying to make somebody believe that he might want to throw a punch at me while wearing a boxing glove."

Trey shook his from side to side. "So...did your dad try to hit you?"

"Yea!" said Little Stevie. "And the rooster didn't like it."

"Ah!" Sighed Trey. "Little Stevie and the guard rooster! Sounds like a book title!"

"Yea well." Little Stevie said at the same time a horn honked outside.

"That's my dad!" Said Trey. "I'll see y'all at school Monday! You need me to do anything else before I go?"

"Nah, we're good. See ya man!"

"Yea, we'll see ya!"

Pretty soon all the cleaning was done and everybody was gone, except for Donald. He and Little Stevie were going fishing in the morning so Donald spent the night.

"You bringing your rooster in the morning?" He asked Little Stevie.

"Yea. Probably. He really hasn't left the house since I brought him home a few weeks ago."

"I guess you don't want a rooster going stir crazy on you. Especially one as big as that one!"

"No, I guess not." Said Little Stevie. He yawned and kissed his mom goodnight and hugged Big Steve. He and Donald went to sleep quickly and six A.M. arrived just as quickly. Both Little Stevie and Donald were up before the alarm sounded however, and they even made up the beds to keep mom from having to do it. Donald went out into the garage to make sure that they had all the tackle they would need to enjoy a good day of fishing and Little Stevie packed up the lunch that his mom had left in the kitchen for them. Little Stevie opened the door to the chicken coop to let the rooster out and they started for the creek.

When they arrived at the spot, it appeared the same as it had when Little Stevie and Big Steve had fished there before. The sun was just rising as the darkness began to disappear and Little Stevie saw a ripple in the water about fifteen feet in front of him. He could see that it was a snake but there wasn't enough light yet for him to tell if it was the same snake as before. "Maybe he'll be back." Little Stevie thought to himself. The rooster saw the snake as well and he was not happy about it. He flapped his wings with his chest stuck out and ruffled up his neck feathers and cackled until the snake was out of sight.

"Let's get some line in the water!" Donald said.

"I hear you man!" Little Stevie replied. "My dad and I did real good the last time we were here. Oh, and by the way, along with a bunch of fish, I caught a snake. And, I saw what could be that *same* snake as soon as we got here, over on the other side of the creek."

"Oh, well I was about to ask you what the rooster got so excited about. I guess it was the snake." Donald said.

"Yea, he doesn't miss much. I could barely see it myself, and he saw it right off."

Donald and Little Stevie got their gear out, baited their hooks with big fat red wigglers and cast their lines into the green water. In only a minute or two Little Stevie got a bite. His bobber began jumping up and down in tiny spurts at first then it disappeared for half a second and reemerged. Donald saw it at the same time as Little Stevie and started coaching him. "Play him Little Stevie." Donald whispered. "He's not ready yet." The rooster sensed the excitement and began pacing back and forth, eyeballing the red and white things bobbing up and down in the water. He watched them disappear and every time they reappeared he squawked.

"I got this man." Little Stevie replied in a whisper too. "You'd better watch your own line." Little Stevie nodded in the direction of Donald's red and white bobber bouncing in and out of the murky water. "Oh crap!" Donald exclaimed. "Oh crap." He repeated in a whisper and turned his attention to his own fishing rod. Little Stevie pulled his catch in first, after a little game of tug-o-war with a nice Largemouth bass that probably weighed at least a pound. And Donald did okay as well by landing another Largemouth bass that didn't weigh as much as the one Little Stevie caught, but put up as much of a fight.

The boys fished for another two hours and caught a total of nine fish, five bass and four catfish, before they decided to call it a day. The sun was shining hot by then and they had already eaten all of the food that mom had packed for them, so they figured it was a good time to call it quits. "Your mom *is* going to fry these here fish up for us, isn't she?" Donald asked as he secured all his gear into his backpack.

'You know it man." Said Little Stevie. "We just gotta get'em to the house before any fish thieves jack us up you know."

"And, she's gonna make those hushpuppies that everybody loves so much. Right?"

"Right!" Said Little Stevie as he secured his equipment.

"Well, what are we waiting for?" Asked Donald.

"What are we...?" Little Stevie began.

"Well, well, well. Look who it is!" Barney said coming out of the woodline. He and three of his "gang" were carrying cane poles and looking mean. "Fishing in our spot too!"

"This is anybody's spot that gets here first!" Donald stood up with a stick in his hand.

"Yea!" Agreed Little Stevie. "So I guess it's a good thing that we were just leaving!"

"We've already caught all the fish that are going to bite today anyway!" Little Stevie added for spite.

"Whatchoo gonna do with that stick?" Barney asked Donald while he continued looking at Little Stevie.

"Whatever I gotta do!" Replied Donald. "So don't make me do anything!"

"You don't tell me what to do!" Barney snapped and moved toward Little Stevie. When he did that the rooster craned his neck and flapped his wings like he was getting ready for a fight. Neither Barney nor any of his thug pals had even seen the rooster for all the brush so when he made his presence known, a couple of the bully buddies shrieked like little girls and almost wet themselves.

"There's our lunch fellas, somebody start a fire!" Barney said with a sneer. Little Stevie couldn't help himself. He was fired up mad and walked straight toward Barney with his fists clenched.

"Oh yea!" Barney said and dropped his rod and tackle to the ground. "Come and git sum!" He thought that his size and meanness would change Little Stevie's mind but it didn't. Little Stevie continued in Barney's direction unafraid of any of them at that moment, and Barney actually got a little nervous because of Little Stevie's boldness. Barney's buddies moved closer to him and barney balled his own fists, getting ready to throw a punch. Little Stevie was almost there and preparing to go toe to toe with his arch enemy and he knew right then that he and Donald were going to get beat up again. There was no way that they could take on all four of them, as big as they were, and come out on top. "Oh well." He thought and began to swing.

"What the crap?" He heard someone cry out. Little Stevie saw Barney turn around to look behind him and he heard a louder, fear filled scream. "Hey, get away from me! Help! Barney!" Little Stevie then saw the kid screaming in fright take off running, with the rooster on his tail. The rooster came back but the kid kept running until he was out of sight. He ran at Barney and his buddies with his wings out full spread and the feathers on his neck ruffled up as high as possible. The three of them panicked and Barney tried to kick the rooster as the other two scooted away from the danger. The rooster ducked in time to avoid Barney's foot, but Barney kicked as hard as he could and he couldn't avoid his other foot coming out from underneath him, sending him flying up in the air. What goes up however, must come down and Barney came down with a thud and a groan as his big rear hit the ground. "Agghh!" Barney moaned on impact. He looked around him for backup but he was all alone. When he got up, still moaning, the first person he saw was Little Stevie and he wanted payback. Barney charged Little Stevie and forgot all about his buddies being gone and, he forgot about the rooster. Little Stevie balled his fists again, waiting for the attack and the whooping he knew he was going to get. Barney was in his face by then and drawing back to swing when all of a sudden a screeching, clucking, black and orange blur flew up in front of Little Stevie's face and he found himself ducking. Barney began screaming for mercy. "Get him off me! Get him off me!" Little Stevie straightened up and saw the rooster three feet off the ground and in Barney's face, giving him a two tone feathered assault. The rooster wasn't hurting Barney, but Barney didn't know that. Little Stevie remembered how his dad had told him that a rooster's spurs *could* hurt somebody however, and even after all that Barney had done to him, he felt sorry for the dim-wit that had a psycho rooster all over him. The rooster hadn't spurred Barney, he really hadn't even touched him except with his wings, and that was only scaring Barney. "Little Stevie!" Get him off me! Please!"

"Just stop moving, and he'll quit!" Said Little Stevie. Little Stevie looked around for Donald and saw him over by the creek. He was rolling with laughter at Barney, and how the others had just left him when the rooster attacked. Little Stevie knelt down in front of Barney and the rooster. "Okay buddy. It's over." Little

Stevie said to the rooster. "Come on. Let's go home." The rooster didn't move. "Barney, quit making such a ruckus and he'll leave you alone! Besides, he hasn't touched you!" Barney stopped screaming like a girl and the rooster went and stood by Little Stevie. "Ya see?" Asked Little Stevie. "You scared him with all that racket."

"We're going to leave now Barney." Donald mocked. "Now, you wait right here until all your friends come back. They should be back any time now. Bye bye now! We'll see you now!" Barney laid there for a few seconds after Little Stevie, Donald and the rooster left. Right at that moment he was sure glad that none of his bully pals were there to see how scared he had been, and he vowed that he was gonna get payback, from Little Stevie!

"Man, those melon heads aren't going to leave you alone." Donald told Little Stevie, after the boys walked half way home in silence "Especially Barney, especially now!"

"It sure looks that way." Replied Little Stevie. "It's getting old too, having to be on the lookout all the time."

"You know, they never really bother *me* unless I'm with you." Donald pointed out.

"Really?" Asked Little Stevie. "I guess you'd better find yourself a new best friend."

"Humph!" Donald snorted. "I'd rather not, if you don't mind. There's not a whole lot to choose from these days. You're the best I could get for the money."

"Yea, but hanging out with me could be hazardous to your health, so maybe you ought to think about it."

"Hey, are you and your dad still training?" Donald asked. "You know, the boxing?"

"Yea. Usually two or three days a week, after supper."

"Well, how's *that* goin?"

"It's going real well, actually." Said Little Stevie. "Dad says that he might even let me compete if I wanted to, if I keep getting better."

"Well, have you thought about just having it out with Barney." Donald asked. "You know, just to get it over with. Just you and him. Maybe he'll leave you alone after that."

"Oh yes. I've given that a lot of thought." Little Stevie said. "And it's going to happen. The question is when. But you never see him without all of his thug friends hangin around so you know it won't be a fair fight."

"Yea, like the last time you and me tangled with them."

"Exactly!" Said Little Stevie.

"How many of them were there? Like Forty?"

"Uh, I think it was more like four or five. And the size difference, you know, we *were* more than outnumbered!"

"I wonder what would be a good way to get Barney away from the rest of the idiots." Donald said. "I've never even seen any of them without at least Barney and one or two others along."

"Well, I'm not going to go out looking for a fight with any of them!" Little Stevie said. "Are you crazy?"

"No. I just thought that if it was bound to happen anyway, you would surprise the crap out of him if you just walked up and started wailing on him."

"Oh yea? And what's to stop the rest of them from helping him tear me apart?" Asked Little Stevie.

"I'm glad you asked that." Said Donald. "Cause I've been thinking. There's strength in numbers right? And there's more of us than there are of them, so we just make out like it's a party and invite everybody we know. I don't think they would be so brave with twenty or thirty people standing around!"

"And just where are we supposed to do this at? If we pull this at school we're bound to get suspended, and my mom would kill me!"

"Yea, I know." Replied Donald. "It was just a thought. Hey, here's another thought. I was wondering about you and Jenny. That was a pretty sweet kiss at the party the other day. Have you talked to her since?"

"Why yes I have, once. We talked for a minute the next day after that."

"Have y'all set a date yet?"

"A date?" Asked Little Stevie. "For what? Oh, you nut!"

"Nah man, I was just kiddin. She *is* a pretty girl though!"

"Yes she is!" Replied Little Stevie with a mile wide grin. "I could do a lot worse."

"Yea, so when are you going to see her again?"

"I don't know. Probably at school."

"What?" Exclaimed Donald. "No. I mean when are y'all going out again?"

"We haven't gone out the first time!" Said Little Stevie. "We just kissed that one time, at the party, on a dare! You're getting way ahead on all this stuff man!"

"Take it easy. I'm just looking out for the best interest of my best bud!"

"Well, let's focus on one thing at a time." Little Stevie told him. "We've got to figure out this Barney thing!"

"What Barney thing? I thought you were just going to try and avoid him for the time being!"

"Well, I'd rather talk about bullies than girls right now. You know, something not so scary!"

"Little Stevie's scared of the chicks!" Donald teased.

"Yea, well, they *can* be a little scary!"

"What?" Exclaimed Donald. "Chicks, scary? What? Well yea, I guess they are!" He

agreed. "Hey, speaking of girls, is it just me or do you sometimes get sick at your stomach when it's just you and a girl, you know, by yourselves, talking and stuff?"

"You ain't alone bro." Said Little Stevie. "You ain't alone!"

chapter one

The boys went to the Baptist church with their families on Sunday, as usual, and then they all had a nice Sunday dinner with their families. The week began on Monday like it always did with Little Stevie and Donald finding themselves getting out of their family cars in the car-rider line at school, usually at about the same time. Little Stevie and Donald walked into the cafeteria together and joined their like minded young peers for some lively conversation about whatever teenaged phenomenon had, or was occurring either that day or sometime already, or later in the week.

"Hey man!" Trey called across the table to Little Stevie. "That party was awesome!"

"Yea, it wasn't too bad. Was it?"

"It was outstanding! You know what else I heard that was pretty cool?" Trey asked.

Little Stevie wrinkled his forehead. "No. What?"

"I heard that Barney cried and screamed like a little girl when your rooster flew up into his face, and just flapped his wings all up in his ugly mug!"

"What? Where did you hear that?" Little Stevie asked Trey.

"It's all over the school man. About how the rooster made Barney cry and scream without even touching him." Trey explained.

"That's just great! I'm dead!" Little Stevie said. "Barney's gonna think that I started that rumor and he's going to finish what he started a while back!"

"Nah, I don't think Barney knows anything about it yet. He and the five stooges have been fairly quiet so far."

Little Stevie risked glancing over at the bully table. He took a quick peek while stretching and wouldn't you know it, his eyes met the mean, dark little beads that were Barney's eyes looking directly at him. "Crap!" He said to himself.

There was one other time that day when Little Stevie had a visual run-in with Barney the Bully. Other than those two eyeball to eyeball confrontations, it was a peaceful day. Little Stevie *did* hear a couple of rumors that Barney was out to get him, and *those* kinds of stories had been going around for months, but Little Stevie knew that it was only a matter of time now, since Barney *did* cry like a little girl, and he *would* think that Little Stevie started that trumor. That's a rumor based on truth, and Barney was gonna want payback for the rooster thing anyway.

When he got home from school however, he wanted to start training right away. "Let's work out before supper time, and again an hour or so afterwards." He told Big Steve.

"Well alright big guy!" Replied Big Steve. "You get changed, and I'll get everything ready. Don't forget your mouthpiece!"

Fifteen minutes later Little Stevie was skipping rope to warm up. After 3, three minute rounds he was sweating like a horse but breathing easy and really focused. Big Steve had noticed a change in Little Stevie's condition since they had first begun training. His punches were sharp and fast, and he was really quick on his feet too. His stamina was greatly improved, and his confidence was at an all time high.

Little finished with his warming up and began wrapping his hands to work the punch mitts. Big Steve put on the punch mitts and gave Little Stevie commands telling him which punches or combinations to throw. "One two! One two! One two three!" Commanded Big Steve, and Little would respond with the proper punches to the mitts covering his father's hands. Or, Big Steve would throw the punches and Little would practice defense and try not to get tagged by any of Big Steve's wide swinging blows. "Slip, slip. Bob and weave now! Move left, and come back around!" Big Steve instructed his son.

Six rounds later and it was time to do push-ups and sit-ups. "Ten at a time. Slow and easy!" Big Steve said. Little Stevie did fifty push-ups, ten at a time, while Big Steve watched with wonder at how much his son had improved since they had started training. Little Stevie was getting stronger and quicker and his skills had improved greatly. Not to mention that nature was taking it's course with Little Stevie and he was developing muscles also. "Those bullies had better be careful about who they pick on these days." Big Steve thought to himself. "They might just get a big surprise next time."

Little Stevie trained like that for several weeks, three or four days a week, and everybody at school noticed that there was something different about him, they just didn't know what it was. Little Stevie never said anything about it to any of his friends or classmates, except for Donald, but he was certainly feeling the changes.

There were days when he was in the right kind of mood that he wished someone would try and pick on him, but they never did. Everybody *liked* Little Stevie, except for the bullies of course, so nobody ever gave Little Stevie a hard time anyway. Except for Barney. He hadn't forgotten about the rooster attack or the shame that followed. The rumors that he had cried and screamed like a girl were all over the school and even his small circle of friends seemed to be growing smaller so Barney was going to have to do something soon to save face. In his tiny little mind everybody was going to think he was a wuss, and he couldn't have that. The more he thought about it, the madder he got, and when Barney got mad he didn't worry about things like rules and getting suspended so he came up with a plan of his own. He knew when Little Stevie had PE, so Barney was going to skip school one day and come to school after the late bell and hide in the locker room. Then he was going to wait for Little Stevie, and the rest of the boys, to come into the locker room when PE was over and he would just beat the snot out of

Little Stevie in front of all the other guys. "Yea!" Barney thought. "That oughtta do it!"

He made the mistake however of telling all his friends about it so when the day came to carry out his ill thought out mission, he had a small crowd skipping school with him. None of them had any idea how it was going to look if they skipped on the same day but they didn't give a lot of thought to anything they did. Three of Barney's bully buddies slinked into the locker room with him while the PE class played softball. About fifteen minutes before the class period was over the PE coach told the class to go and clean up and get ready for next period.

"They're coming now!" Barney's buddy Tom hissed as he stood in the locker room door.

"Okay, everybody hide in the shower until they're all in here!" Barney said. "Then I'm gonna kick Little Stevie's butt!"

"You go boy!" Said Tom as he remained in the doorway. "Give him one for me!" He added with his hands on either side of the doorway.

"Tom!" Barney screeched. "Get in here and close the door, they're coming!" He heard the hallway door slam and the sound of footsteps down the hall.

The four of them hid themselves in the shower and waited until they heard the door to the locker room open and the bustling of kids hurrying to get undressed. Then Barney heard the voice of his arch enemy, Little Stevie.

"Hey Donald, did you bring any deodorant? I couldn't find mine."

"Yea!" Donald replied. "I got some. Brand new too. Still got the plastic wrapped around the top."

By then all the boys were in the locker room so Barney and his gang of thugs stepped out of the shower.

"Well, well, well!" Barney said. "Somebody's gonna need more than doderant when I'm done. I'm gonna beat the crap out you Little Stevie!"

Every head in the locker room turned when Barney spewed his garbage, especially Little Stevie. He stared at Barney, and when two of his bully buddies went over and stood in front of the door, he was scared, but only a second. He knew then that he could take Barney and he felt the fear being replaced by another emotion. Anger! Little Stevie felt it bubbling up inside of him, but he remembered what Big Steve had taught him along with all the training. "Keep your cool." Big Steve had told him more than once. "Let the other guy get mad and lose control, and you'll beat him every time." So that's what he did. He remained calm, even when Tom and the other bully had stopped Donald and another kid from leaving to go get their PE coach. They blocked the door and dared anyone to leave and most of the kids were intimidated at first so they just stood by their lockers, half dressed.

Not Little Stevie. He remembered everything his dad had taught him, and he intended to put it to good use. First, he thought he would have some fun with Barney though.

"Barney!" He said so suddenly and loudly that it jolted everybody, including Barney. "Am I going to have to stomp just *your* guts out, or all four of you?"

"What?" Barney asked. He was about to say something stupid but Little Stevie was feeling bold.

"And what the crap is doderant?" He asked while he slowly walked across the locker room toward Barney.

Barney began looking around at his buddies and all of a sudden he wasn't so sure of himself anymore. In fact, he was getting a little nervous. He couldn't back down however, this was something *he* started.

"What?" He asked again. He began shifting his weight from one foot to the other.

"Doderant!" Little Stevie repeated. "That's what you said when you came in wasn't it? You know, just before you said you were going to beat the crap out of me! Who is your English teacher anyway?" He asked with a confident grin on his face. "I don't think you're learning anything in that class!"

Little Stevie stopped a few feet from Barney. Barney was as confused as he was scared at that moment and he looked over at Tom and the other one by the door and then at his third buddy. All three started toward Little Stevie but stopped in their tracks when Donald jumped up from the locker room bench and stood by Little Stevie.

"I got your back bro!" He said, glaring at the bullies with his fists clenched and up, in front of his face. Then, another one of Little Stevie's friends stepped up and said the same thing. Before long all of the kids were standing with Little Stevie and Donald and the bullies didn't know what to do. There must have been fifteen or more guys behind Little Stevie and they all meant business. Six of them moved over to the door and stood behind Tom and the other one. They nervously glanced at the six guys behind them, sighed and backed off. The third bully sat down on the bench, looked at Barney and just shrugged.

"Are you still gonna beat the crap out of me Barney?" Little Stevie asked with a hint of sarcasm in his voice. "It's just you and me now! Oh, listen to my grammer!" He said. "I'm sorry, it's just you and *I* now!" He picked up Donald's stick of deodorant. "Are you sweating yet?" He asked, getting bolder by the second. "Are you nervous?" Barney simply stood there with a blank look on his face.

"Well?" Little Stevie asked with his arms out in front of him and his palms up. Big Steve had taught him that also, to always be ready for a surprise attack. That's just what Barney had in mind too, a surprise attack. Without warning he charged at Little Stevie. "Aagghh!" He screamed as he ran toward Little Stevie with his head down. Little Stevie quickly stepped to the side and

Barney flew right by him still looking at the floor. He ran headfirst into a locker and bounced off of it. He then fell back onto the floor, more embarrassed than hurt, but now in a rage that was focused on Little Stevie. He got up and charged again but stopped just short of running into Little Stevie. He put up his fists and began to swing at Little Stevie's head. There were "oohs" and an "oh no" out of concern for Little Stevie but then there were some "dangs" and some "wows" after Little Stevie slipped, bobbed and weaved his way out of getting hammered by Barney's fat fists. Barney swung a wild right hook at Little Stevie and Little Stevie simply bent his knees and the punch went right over his head. Barney however, starting spinning like a ballet dancer, until he spun around three hundred sixty degrees and once again hit the floor. The frustration on his face was obvious as he made one last ditch effort to hit Little Stevie. He came up swinging again but Little Stevie was ready. He launched a left jab at Barney's nose and it landed with a crunch. Barney's head rocked backward and there was complete silence for just a second. Barney wasn't used to being the one getting punched and none of the kids in the locker room, including the bully buddies, had ever seen Barney on the receiving end of a one. Barney was getting his butt handed to him on a plate and he wanted to run away, but everybody was looking at him now and he had no choice but to keep on keeping on. Little Stevie only made things worse with what he said next. "Don't make me hurt you Barney!" He said. "Let's just stop this right now!"

Barney was furious. He tried once more to clobber Little Stevie with his wild, hammer like blows, but it was no use. Little Stevie nailed him in the nose again with a hard right hand and Barney sat down. Right there on the floor he just sat down, stunned by the punch he had just taken directly in the face. He shook his head and tried to get back up, but Little Stevie hit him again, this time in the eye. Barney collapsed onto his back and laid there, dazed and really confused. Tom and the other bullies made a move in Little Stevie's direction and as soon as they did, they were surrounded by fifteen kids who were tired of being picked on and terrorized by the small group of would be criminals. It didn't matter though, right then Little Stevie would have fought every one of them.

"Y'all going somewhere?" Donald asked them and they froze in their tracks.

Tom looked on either side of him, at the big group outnumbering his small group. "Yea man." Tom said. "We're just going to help Barney up, and then we're gonna get out of here!"

Donald looked at Little Stevie. "You done man?"

"That depends on him." He pointed at Barney. "You done with all this craziness Barney?"

Barney sat up and shook his head again, but before he could say anything Little Stevie added. "And I mean for good. I'm not going to take your crap anymore. Do you understand?"

Barney sat there, still dazed by what just happened. Then he looked up at Little Stevie with a confused look on his face, like he didn't speak English.

"Answer me!" Little Stevie demanded with his fists clenched.

Barney flinched from fear, but finally nodded. "Yea Little Stevie, I'm done. I just wanna get outta here." He said.

Little Stevie gazed at Barney the bully for a couple of seconds and then stuck out his hand down to Barney. Barney appeared really confused when he looked it, but then he grabbed it and let Little Stevie help him up. He almost fell back to the floor from dizziness but Little Stevie held him up. Little Stevie let go of Barney's hand, then turned away.

"Okay then." He said. "I guess we're done here."

As they were leaving the locker room Little Stevie and Donald both got pats on the back from their classmates. "Good job guys!" and "Way to go!" Were just a few of the praises they heard.

"Man, I didn't do anything." Donald pointed out to them. "Little Stevie did all the work. I was just there, like all of you guys!"

"Nah Donald." Said Little Stevie. "I *was* a little scared, and you had my back. I appreciate it."

"Well I wasn't going to just stand there and watch you get jumped by four guys!"

"That's what I mean!" Replied Little Stevie. "You had my back, in case."

"Well, I'm glad you didn't make his nose bleed." Said Donald. "If it had bled, that would have been hard to explain to Mr. Flannagan. Especially after the last time we were in his office."

"I don't think so." Little Stevie said. "I think Barney skipped school today, remember? They weren't in the cafeteria this morning. And, don't forget the little chat our dads had with the principal."

"Oh yea, that's right. They *did* put the fear of God into him." Donald replied. "And it would have been kinda hard for Barney to explain why they were here during PE class and not in home-room this morning."

"Yea, especially when they were in *our* PE class!" Replied Little Stevie.

"Hey man, do you think your dad would mind if I trained with you a few times?" Donald asked as they walked.

"Of course not Donald. You're my best bud. You're welcome anytime."

"That would be awesome man, if I could do what you just did to Barney. I mean he didn't know whether to crap or go blind!" Donald exclaimed in his excited, high pitched voice. Little Stevie thought he sounded like a girl.

"Hey man, don't do that!" He told Donald.

"Don't do what?"

"Get all excited and start talking in your squeaky voice. I told you that you sound like a girl when you do that."

"I'll show *you* a girl!" Donald said. "Gut sum! Come on, git sum!" Donald put up his fists like they were going to fight. They slap boxed for a few seconds and went to next period.

When Little Stevie arrived at his next class the news of what happened in the locker room had already gotten there. Little Stevie and Donald had told everybody that was in the locker room not to say anything about it but they were almost certain that the story would be told. They just didn't know how fast the news would travel. It seemed to be confined to the students however, since not a single faculty member had asked him about it. All the kids in his class were giving him looks though. They were making thumbs up signs and giving him okay signals. Some even asked him for his autograph. He felt like a celebrity but at the same time he felt a little bit sorry for Barney. "He's just like a dumb animal." Little Stevie thought to himself. "Humph!"

Later on, in the car rider line Little Stevie was looking for Barney, but he figured that Barney had probably gone back home. He wondered if Barney was going to be in trouble for skipping school, but then he realized that nobody at school would have missed him and more than likely nobody at his house paid any attention to anything he did. Little Stevie decided not to tell his parents about the fight and when his mom picked him up he tried to act normal. His mom could tell however that he was really excited about something.

"So, how was *your* day today son?" Mom asked as she pulled out of the car rider line.

"Oh, it was okay." Little Stevie said. "Did you have a good day today mom?" Little Stevie asked with a wide grin on his face. He was looking out the passenger side window though, so mom couldn't see his face.

"Why yes I did Stevie. Thank you for asking."

He didn't say anything else and mom didn't want to pressure him. She knew if he had something important to say he would tell her or Big Steve when he was ready. When they arrived home he went out to the chicken coop and let the rooster out for a while. Little Stevie told his mom that he and the rooster were going to take a walk and that he would be back in a little while.

"He's been cooped up all day mom, he needs some exercise." Little Stevie told her.

"Well, okay." Mom said. "Just be home before supper! And be careful!" She called out.

"I will!"

He and the rooster walked over to Donalds house. Donald was taking out the garbage when Little Stevie arrived with the rooster right beside him.

"Hey man!" Donald greeted him. "Oh, I mean, hey Rocky. You bust anybody up lately, since the last time I saw you?"

"As a matter of fact," He began. "Uh, no. Not since the last one." He and Donald laughed. "You know, I was scared to death at first. With Barney I mean. I knew you had my back, but I had no idea that the rest of the guys were gonna stand up to that bunch like *you all* did."

"Neither did I!" Donald replied. "At first I thought it was gonna be just you and me, and I would have probably gotten my butt kicked, but I was going down swinging."

"I hear you man. But you know, I don't think we have to worry too much about Barney and his gang anymore. I mean everybody was ready to start throwing down on that bunch, and I don't think they're going to forget about that for a while!"

"You got *that* right!" Exclaimed Donald. I haven't seen anybody *that* scared since uh, uh, Mr Flannagan that day when your dad and mine put him in his place!"

"Yea!" Little Stevie scoffed. "He didn't know whether he was afoot or horseback!"

"Yea man!" Said Donald. "What?" He shook his head.

"It's just something I've heard my Paw Paw say. Forget it."

"You don't know what it means either. Do you?"

"Uh, no." Little Stevie confessed.

"Well, in that case, let's go fishing this Saturday. In celebration of uh, what your Paw Paw said."

"Sounds like a plan Stan."

"Hey, and bring your friend there." Donald said and pointed at the rooster.

"Definitely!" Said Little Stevie. "I've been keeping him penned up too much lately. I told my mom already that he needed some exercise earlier so we walked way over here."

"Well good. Maybe he'll bring us good luck." Donald replied. "And he's sure to get some exercise. That's a pretty good walk."

"*Yea* it is! We'll all get little sweat rolling!"

Sure enough, when Saturday came along, Little Stevie and Donald both were dripping sweat while they followed their trail to the creek. It was hard to tell if the rooster was sweating, but neither Little Stevie nor Donald knew if roosters even sweated.

It was all part of life though, the sweating, the walking, the carrying of gear and food and the constantly looking around for snakes and other creatures that would bite you or sting you if they had the chance. It was all part of the process, and part of the discovering, the learning, the growing up and the making of memories to be cherished one day, years down the road.

Just like the fishing trip the boys were on. They had been fishing in the same spot many times, but *that* day would turn out to be one of the most memorable fishing days the two of them would ever experience. Everything seemed normal enough when they started out. All was calm as the first cast was made and Little Stevie was already getting a bite.

"Look out!" Little Stevie whispered excitedly. "*I got one already!*"

"Well, play him Little Stevie. Don't let him get ahead of you there!"

"I got this Bro-man!" Little Stevie replied.

"I know. I know." Said Donald. "Just don't get in a hurry and lose him!"

The rooster sensed the excitement in Little Stevie's voice so he got into it as well. He screeched and flapped his wings and cut loose with a cock-a-doodle-do. Then he began to pace back and forth and cackle as the boys focused on the fish at the end of Little Stevie's line. "There you go." Donald was saying. "Pull him in easy. Slow and easy."

"Aw man!" Little Stevie exclaimed. "Look at that sucker! I'll bet he weighs three pounds!" Little Stevie reeled the fish in and it was one of the biggest catfish he'd ever caught in the creek.

"Man!" Donald said. "Meat on the table! That whale would make two men a good meal!"

Donald was admiring Little Stevie's catch and didn't notice the jerking of his own rod when a monster bass gobbled up the bait, and the hook. The fishing rod simply bent downward at first but then the entire fishing pole, reel and all, began moving in the direction of the water. It was being dragged into the murky green depths by a killer whale of a Big Mouth Bass that seemed determined to make a getaway with as much free stuff as he could. Donald finally saw his fishing rod and everything attached to it leap off the creek bank and into the water. By the time he reached the edge of the bank his fishing gear had been dragged to the other side of the creek bank and was sinking rapidly. The water wasn't deep however, only about three feet at it's deepest point, and the rod and reel were new so Donald wasn't about to let them go that easily.

"Pull your line in Little Stevie. I'm going to get mine back!" He said boldly and took off his sneakers.

"Wait for me!" Little Stevie said. Donald was already in the water, splashing around like a sea lion and he was nowhere near his fishing rod. Little Stevie was right behind him, chest deep in no time and looking for maximum depth. Their fishing day had evolved into a swimming day and that was alright because it had been a scorcher. The relief from the cool creek water was visible on the boys faces as they splashed each other, did back flips off the bank and took turns diving to see which one could hold their breath the longest. Every once in awhile one of them would grab hold of the other one's foot and pull him under.

Little Stevie decided to let his fish go since they probably weren't going to fish anymore, and Donald did the same. The cool creek water had the desired effect so the boys swam/walked across to the other side to retrieve the lost equipment. Once they secured everything they sat down on the bank and just gazed into the pea green water.

"Hey, look at my rooster!" He told Donald. The rooster was pacing. He wasn't going very far in one direction or the other, he was simply going one way for a few steps, and then turning and going the other way for a few steps. He also let out a few cackles and even appeared to be looking for something to come out of the woods.

"What's wrong with him?" Donald asked. "Does he do that a lot?"

"Only when he gets excited or when something's about to happen." Little Stevie replied. "Maybe it's just because we're way over here, on the other side of the creek. I don't know what else would be bothering him."

As soon as Little Stevie finished talking the rooster stopped pacing and stared at the woodline. "Uh oh!" Little Stevie said. "He sees something!"

It was the fox! And not just any fox, but the one that Plowboy Jack had told him about. It was orange with black feet and Little Stevie could see that it was missing a piece of his right ear. His head and shoulders appeared out of the bushes and it stopped, peering at the rooster. That's why the rooster stopped as well. He sensed the presence of the fox before he saw it, and now it was right in front of him, getting ready to attack. The staredown seemed to go on forever. Little Stevie and Donald were frozen in awe of the scene and didn't know what to do or what might happen if they did anything.

"That's the fox that killed Plowboy Jack's chickens and almost killed my rooster!"

"How do you know that?" Donald asked in a whisper.

"Because!" He said. "Plowboy Jack told me that I couldn't miss this one. He described him to me." He added. "You see that chunk missing out of his ear? Well Plowboy Jack said that..." The fox charged the rooster! "Oh crap!" Exclaimed Little Stevie. Before he could move, the fox was upon the rooster and it looked like he was going to finish what he had started months ago. The fox opened it's mouth to bite and just before it slammed into him, the rooster flapped it's wings and flew straight up in the air, almost three feet. The fox continued in the direction it was going and ran into an Oak tree, headfirst. The fox shook its head and hissed. Then it turned around to face the rooster who was back on the ground and ready. The fox charged again and Little Stevie gasped in fear for his rooster, but once again the rooster surprised Little Stevie, Donald and the fox. The rooster flapped it's wings again and lifted himself off the ground only to come back down on the foxes back. The fox hissed and let out a yelp of pain when the rooster squeezed with his talons and dug into the fox's flesh. The fox began spinning to get the rooster off his back. It looked like a small dog that was chasing it's tail and trying to bite the fleas that were biting *him.* It spun so fast that it got dizzy and bit it's own tail. The fox yelped in painful surprise and jumped off the ground with all four feet. When it came back down it landed on it's back but the rooster had already jumped off and onto a rock. He flapped his wings and let out a crow that stopped the fox in it's tracks as it was charging once again. After a couple of seconds of confusion however, it resumed the charge. The fox was almost upon him again and at the same time that it jumped toward the rock, the rooster took off like a rocket with a wing boost and if foxes had chins, that one would have busted *his* on the top of that rock. He was stunned worse than before and it took a second longer for him to recover. Meanwhile the rooster was strutting around and scratching up a storm of dust and leaves and believe it or not the fox started hacking and coughing from all the debris sailing through the air. He wasn't completely done however, and ran full steam at the rooster one more time. That fox was determined to have chicken for supper, but at the last second he stopped just short of the dinner table. He remembered what happened the last couple of times he ran head first at that rooster so he stopped and waited for the rooster to fly up and away, like he'd done before. The rooster didn't try to avoid the fox this time, he went on the offensive. When the fox came to a full stop, the rooster charged *him* with both wings flapping wildly until he was close enough to try and "spur" the fox. The fox went low and tried to snatch one of the rooster's legs and when he did, the rooster left the ground with some rapid beating of some strong wings. The rooster shifted his weight and came down on the fox's shoulder with one of his spurs. It only nicked him but he let loose with a cry of pain and spun around to bite whatever it was that was causing him pain. The fox lunged forward and as his teeth were closing down on what he thought was going to be dinner, he got a mouthful of air. The rooster charged right back at the fox and totally surprised him with more wing beating, which actually scared the fox more than it hurt him, but then he reared up once again to use his deadly spurs. The rooster used his God given weapon like a sword and whacked another piece of the fox's ear off. He yelped louder than before and shook his head violently while the rooster was preparing for another attack. The rooster moved around behind the fox and charged like a mad bull. He was screeching and cackling and beating his wings and the noise was something awful. It took the fox by surprise again and the fox was tired of surprises. He made an escape attempt, but just before he got his back legs moving, the rooster pecked him, good and hard on the back of his hind leg. The fox howled like he'd been shot, and he shot out of there like a rocket! The rooster followed after the fox for only a few feet, then returned to the creek bank, walking slowly and making those rooster noises that sound like a rusty hinge.

"Wow!" Said Donald. He and Little Stevie both stood in awe of what they just saw with their own eyes. With their mouths as wide open as their eyes, the boys stared across the creek at the rooster. "That was the most incredible thing I have ever seen!"

Little Stevie looked at the rooster, then at Donald. He repeated that several times before he spoke. "Tell me about it! I just wish we had a video camera, cause nobody's gonna believe this!"

The rooster flapped it's wings and crowed proudly as the boys waded back across the creek. The fox was nowhere in sight and the only sign that a life or death struggle had occurred by the creek that day was a little piece of a fox's ear. The boys stepped over it without noticing as they were leaving and the rooster led the way home, strutting proudly like he was king of the world.

CPSIA information can be obtained
at www.ICGtesting.com
Printed in the USA
BVHW080338091118
532591BV00003B/4/P

9 781545 611548